# IT BEGAN WITH A KISS

## A MEDIEVAL ROMANCE

### THE MACLARENS: BOOK FOUR

## SHERRY EWING

KINGSBURG PRESS

Kingsburg Press
P.O. Box 475146
San Francisco, CA 94147
www.KingsburgPress.com

*It Began With A Kiss* is a work of fiction. Names, characters, places, and incidents are a product of the author's imagination. Locales and public names are sometimes used for atmospheric purposes. Any resemblance to actual people, living or dead, or to businesses, companies, events, institutions, or locales is completely coincidental.

Editor: Jude Knight
Front Cover Design: Bookcoverzone.com

*It Began With A Kiss*/Sherry Ewing -- 1st ed
ISBN eBook: 978-1-946177-69-8
ISBN Print: 978-1-946177-70-4

ISBN Expanded Distribution: 978-1-946177-71-1
ISBN Barnes & Noble Print: 978-1-946177-72-8

Library of Congress Control Number: 2023913280

# OTHER BOOKS BY SHERRY EWING

## Medieval & Time Travel Series

*To Love A Scottish Laird:* De Wolfe Pack

Connected World

*To Love An English Knight:* De Wolfe Pack

Connected World

*If My Heart Could See You:* The MacLarens (Book One)

*For All of Ever*: The Knights of Berwyck,

A Quest Through Time (Book One)

*Only For You*: The Knights of Berwyck,

A Quest Through Time (Book Two)

*Hearts Across Time:* The Knights of Berwyck,

A Quest Through Time (Books One & Two)

A special box set of For All of Ever & Only For You

*A Knight To Call My Own:* The MacLarens (Book Two)

*To Follow My Heart:* The Knights of Berwyck,

A Quest Through Time (Book Three)

*The Piper's Lady:* The MacLarens (Book Three)

*Love Will Find You:* The Knights of Berwyck,

A Quest Through Time (Book Four)

*One Last Kiss:* The Knights of Berwyck,

A Quest Through Time (Book Five)

*Promises Made At Midnight:* The Knights of Berwyck,
A Quest Through Time (Book Six)

*It Began With A Kiss*: The MacLarens (Book Four)

**Regency**

*A Kiss for Charity:* A de Courtenay Novella (Book One)

*The Earl Takes A Wife: A de Courtenay Novella (Book Two)*

*Before I Found You:* A de Courtenay Novella (Book Three)

*Nothing But Time:* A Family of Worth: Book One

*One Moment In Time:* A Family of Worth, Book Two

*Under the Mistletoe*

*A Mistletoe Kiss* in the Bluestocking Belles boxset *Belles & Beaux*
(2022)

*A Second Chance At Love*

*A Countess to Remember*

*To Claim A Lyon's Heart:* Lyon's Den Connected World

Learn more about Sherry's books on her website at www.
SherryEwing.com/books

Join Sherry's newsletter at http://bit.ly/2vGrqQM

# IT BEGAN WITH A KISS

# DEDICATION

*For Diane N.*

Your patience and continued support while you waited for years for me to finish this story has been appreciated. I hope you enjoy Aiden's story. This one is for you!

# CHAPTER 1

*The Year of Our Lord's Grace, 1183*
*Summer, Dunborough Castle, Scotland*

child's laughter rang out in the early evening breeze giving testament to the boy's delight as he made his way along a narrow path. Lady Iona Ferguson followed alongside her husband and laird, Ewan, a basket with the remains from their picnic swinging from the crook of her arm. Their young son Gregor ran ahead, picking up several small rocks and tossing them over the edge of the cliff they traipsed upon.

"Be careful, lad." Iona shouted to be heard over the roaring surf below.

Her husband chuckled. "Ach, Iona, ye coddle the boy too much. He is doing naught but what all young boys his age is doing."

"He is a mischievous imp and ye know it."

"He is nine summers, lass. Of course, he is mischievous."

She playfully punched her husband in the arm, but he only laughed again. 'Twas not as though she could hurt the brute, Ewan's arm being heavily muscled along with the rest of him. "I have the feeling our son has inherited that trait from his father," she murmured gazing up into the face of the tall Scot before her.

Iona had married the laird of Dunborough Castle, a much older man than herself. Not that she was old at a score and eight. They had said their marriage vows and, before she had time to feel married, she was pregnant. But no matter their difference in age, she had come to love her husband. How could she not? Ewan was a handsome man, with his dark hair peppered with hints of grey, and a devoted husband and father. She could not ask for much more than that.

His brown eyes twinkled with merriment when he leaned down to kiss her. "Aye, wife. Gregor does me proud, he does. I only wish we could have another so as tae ensure my name lives on long after I am gone."

Iona linked her arm with Ewan's. The weight of having one child to inherit Dunborough weighed heavily on her mind. She was unsure why she could not conceive again but she would leave it to God to decide if they were to be blessed with more children. "I do not think I could stand more than two of ye cut from the same cloth in our keep, my laird," she teased, hugging his arm close. "Besides, I could always give ye a wee daughter. What would ye be thinking then when her suiters came tae call once she was of an age tae marry?"

"Bah! They would need tae prove their worth, of course," he muttered, even whilst he unconsciously reached for the hilt of the sword that swung from his side.

The sound of falling rocks interrupted their teasing of one another. They looked up in shock to see their son dangling precariously close on the edge of the cliff.

"Gregor!" they yelled in unison and Ewan quickly lessened the distance between them. Grabbing Gregor by the scruff of his shirt, he hauled the boy back to land on even feet upon the treacherous footpath.

Iona sunk to the ground in relief, hiding her tears of concern in her hands. She hated the way to the castle, but this narrow spit of land between the mainland and sea was the only real access to their home. Sometimes Iona wished she still resided in her own humble cottage within the nearby village, but her status had changed drastically when she had married the laird of Dunborough Castle.

'Twas easy to understand why no one ever invaded the castle rising upon the rock formation at the edge of sea. No one in their right mind would attempt to climb the dangerous cliff, and the narrow path between the mainland and the gate of the castle was not meant for an invading army. The knights guarding the keep could see for miles around, so sneaking up on its inhabitants was not likely.

"Mama, I am fine. Ye need not fret," Gregor said, coming to kneel at her side. His small hands took hers, but she could tell he was also trembling in fright.

She grabbed her son, giving him a shake before pulling him down into her lap. "Ye shall be the death of me, sweet Gregor," she proclaimed and began smothering her son with kisses.

"Ma! I am too old for ye tae be treating me like a small bairn," Gregor protested. The boy gave her a fast hug before he

3

took himself from her arms, running ahead to disappear inside the open postern gate.

Ewan held out his hand and Iona was pulled from the ground and into his arms. "Ye canna continue tae show such affection tae the lad, wife. He will be ridiculed by all the other boys his age."

"He almost fell off the cliff, Ewan. That is enough tae be concerned for his welfare."

"Aye, concern, for ye are his mother, but beyond that ye must refrain so the boy will grow tae be a fine warrior. Now come, let us get inside our gates before they close for the eve. If ye remember, I invited my brother Broden to the keep. I have a matter of import tae discuss with him. I am sure he is anxiously waiting in my solar for our return."

Iona brushed the dirt from her gown and looked ahead to the castle. There were times when she hated this place, despite the fact she now called the castle home. "I wish we could have stayed at my old lodgings. Times seemed so much simpler than now, especially when I must needs remind myself that I am lady of the keep."

"We should give the place tae one of the neighbors who are in need of finer dwellings, but I promised ye that we could keep yer lodgings since it made ye happy."

"*Ye* make me happy, Ewan," she replied but her concern must have shown on her face since he halted their progress and lifted her chin to stare into her eyes.

"What is troubling ye, Iona," he whispered, brushing her lips with his thumb.

"I shouldna say anything."

"Voicing yer opinion never stopped ye before. Tell me what is on yer mind, wife."

Iona gave a weary sigh. "I know Broden is yer brother but I like not how he stares at me when he knows ye are not watching."

Ewan chuckled and took her arm as they began to walk. "Broden is one of the most carefree people I know. Ye are imagining such nonsense, Iona. Let the matter rest and let us away," he replied good naturedly.

"I like not staying under the same roof as Broden. Ye may say my thoughts are nonsense but I know what I see," she huffed, even as the gate behind her closed with a loud clang of a metal bolt being put into place.

They both turned to stare at the door. When Ewan looked down upon her and saw her concern, he appeared to be pondering her words. "Mayhap ye have a point."

"'Tis about time ye listen to me."

"I listen," he grumbled.

"Not always but that matters not, at least for now," Iona said. They made their way into the kitchen that normally would be bursting with activity. 'Twas oddly silent. She set the basket down on a table and they continued to make their way through the keep until they reached their bedchamber.

Ewan went to the hearth and began building a fire to take the chill from the room. Once a blaze began to heat the chamber, he stood and looked over his wife. "I will not be long."

"Do ye promise?" she asked, shivering with the thought of being anywhere near her brother-in-law. His outside appearance always appeared happy enough but there was something about the man that set her on edge whenever he was around.

Warm arms enveloped her and she rested her head upon her husband's chest to hear his steady heartbeat. "Aye, Iona. I promise I will not be long."

With a quick kiss, he left the chamber, leaving Iona to wrap her arms around herself. Hours later, Iona was still waiting for him as she stood in the shadows of the room, too worried to even bother to keep the fire lit in the hearth. She had the oddest premonition that tonight would turn her world in a completely different direction than the way she lived now.

# CHAPTER 2

*A*iden of Clan MacLaren peered above his head into the darkness to find his next handhold. He must have lost his wits to be attempting to climb a cliff in the dead of the night. The rocks bit into the palm of his hands whilst he pulled himself up onto the next fragment of narrow ledge that gave purchase for his feet. *The things I do for king and country*, he angrily mused. An English king could grant him much, if he was to overtake this stronghold, but his Scottish roots warred within him, knowing he would be considered a traitor in the eyes of his father's ancestors.

Memories assailed him as Aiden continued his climb. He could in no way condemn his twin sister for falling in love with the very enemy who had laid siege to Berwyck Castle many years ago. Berwyck should have rightfully belonged to him. Yet, what had that siege left him except no title, nor lands to call his own? Everything had been stripped from him and his need to make his own way in the world had caused Aiden to leave Berwyck some time ago. A brief visit here or there was all he could bear, considering all he had lost.

He puzzled over how long his absence from his homeland had truly been. He had always come back, however. Home was home. His sister, Amiria, was happily married. He and Dristan had come to a common accord. Besides, they now had children and Aiden could never stay away for long. He wanted to be able to spoil his nephew and niece whenever the chance arose.

Aiden shook the memories from his mind and once more peered at the rising obstacle before him. He must needs make haste else his plan would all go awry. He had chosen only his sword and a dirk in this attempt to gain access to Dunborough. The weight of his heavy chainmail would only hinder his ascent and there was a need for speed. Hence, he was attired only in tunic and hose. He felt naked and vulnerable, yet there was no time for regrets. He must needs gain entry and reach the hidden postern gate before being discovered. His men awaited the opening of the door.

Hand over hand, he began again, quietly inching his way upwards like a spider climbing a silken thread in order to capture his prey. He slipped, and his bare feet scraped along a rock until he found his footing once more. He knew the routine of the castle. He knew when the guards would change their posts. Had he not been watching closely, these many weeks, for such an opportunity as tonight? No moon would shine down upon him this eve. Nay, the overhead clouds would only add to his concealment and gain him that which he sought. An easy entry, with little to no bloodshed. Or so he would hope.

No one in their right mind would be looking for someone to

scale the side of the steep cliff in order to gain access into the security of the castle walls. Only a fool would risk such an endeavor and Aiden was beginning to doubt his own sanity yet again whilst he balanced at such dizzying heights. Dunborough was, for the most part, sitting on an island with only a small stretch of narrow land connecting it to the mainland of Scotland. Most would look for an attack from the barbican gate and not from an enemy in the interior. He only hoped that the laird of the keep, Ewan Ferguson, would not be vigilant to Aiden's actions.

At long last, he reached the top. Hoisting himself up and over the wall, he slid down into the castle grounds and wasted only a few moments to catch his breath, leaning against the very wall that could have been the end of him. Overhead, he heard the knights walking along the narrow parapet whilst they changed their positions, their clinking chainmail muffled any noise he may have made.

*Crunch, crunch, crunch!* The out of place noise made Aiden reach for his dirk. He peered above him into the darkness. There, sitting on the edge of the wall just as nonchalantly as he could please, was the silhouette of a lad of no more than ten summers. Swinging one leg, he was carelessly perched on the very edge that had almost been Aiden's downfall. *Crunch!* The boy bit into his apple again all the while keeping his eyes trained on him as though he had not a care in the world.

He finished his apple and tossed the core over the side. "'Tis a long way down," he whispered, wiping the juice from his chin with his sleeve. Did the lad actually hold back a laugh? "Thought ye were a goner 'bout halfway up, I did."

"Did not your mother ever tell you to not talk to strangers?"

Aiden asked in disbelief that all his plans could go astray with just one shout out from a small wee lad.

The boy shrugged, all the while studying him. "I only stayed tae see if ye would manage the cliff or ye would plummet tae yer death. I truly dinnae think ye were gonna make it, but here ye are."

"Come here, boy," Aiden urged, wondering if he could get a hold of the lad. He had gumption he did. A trait Aiden could admire but not at the cost of sounding an alarm.

This time boy did indeed laugh out loud. "I dinnae think so."

Before Aiden could reply or make a grab for the child, the lad took off into the night causing Aiden to begin running. He knew an alarm would sound at any moment once the youth told the knights above of his ploy.

On silent feet, he raced near the perimeter of the walls until he reached the gate. With little effort or noise, he opened the door and silently motioned to the dozen men who had accompanied him. The fact these knights had made it thus far was a testament of how silently they had approached the castle one at a time in the dead of night.

Aiden rose two fingers to gesture at his eyes, then pointed toward the parapet. Four men, just as quietly, detached themselves from the group and disappeared into the eve to capture the knights above who were on guard. Another held out Aiden's boots and chainmail. Quickly he slipped on the boots and accepted assistance with donning the heavy protection over his tunic.

Ready to do battle, Aiden and his men silently made their way into the keep. He needed to apprehend the laird who was responsible for this land and place him under guard. Aiden prayed the man would see reason, although he had his doubts since he himself would not easily give up that which was under his care.

They began creeping through the passageways, silently opening doors, looking for Ewan but only espying empty rooms. This was one part of his plan that he knew was dangerous, for how was he to know who occupied which chambers when he did not know the inside workings of the castle? The outside, aye, but nary the interior. Now that he and his men were within, Aiden knew time was of the essence. One more mistake could alert and rouse the keep's inhabitants of an attack. He could not afford the chaos that would surely ensue.

'Twas as if fate decided to point out the stupidity of his thoughts as the tower bell sounded the alarm. One mistake had been enough, the damn child! No sooner had he taken a step towards the next chamber than the door he was about to reach out for was pulled open. A shriek rent the air and Aiden, without haste, clamped his hand upon the person's mouth.

"Find him," Aiden ordered. He gave a jerk of his head and his men wasted no time in their attempt to find Laird Ewan. There was now no need to remain quiet. Their moment of opportunity was lost as Aiden heard his men drawing their swords down the corridor.

Sharp teeth sank into his hand. "God's blood," Aiden cursed, shoving the person back into the chamber and slamming the door. Shaking his hand to get some feeling back into his bruised fingers, he barely ducked in time to miss the iron poker from the hearth that was aimed at his head. He must be losing his edge if he did not see that one coming.

His assailant's shadow moved across the dimly lit room like

a specter from the underworld wanting to lay claim to his soul. But Aiden's mission was just, and he was in no way prepared to meet an early demise. Nay, no one would halt his mission to become victorious with the rising sun, including the person who began throwing any object in his direction.

"Cease your madness," Aiden warned, only to dodge a heavy chalice that ricocheted off the wall. By damned, enough was enough.

Aiden advanced with an angry stride, causing another shriek of outrage to erupt from the person he stalked. But the chamber was not overly large and there was no place to hide from Aiden's growing wrath. His quarry was trapped in the darkest corner of the room. Without further thought, Aiden leaped forward. A knife slashed through the air. Aiden whirled, wrapping his arm around the person's waist, but not before he felt blood beginning to run down his arm. He tightened his hold and his senses immediately gave him surprising news about the person he was holding.

There could be no mistake. This was a woman, for her curves were intimately molded to his body, and Aiden certainly knew when there was a lady within his arms. Her hair was trapped between them and the flowery fragrance of her tresses made Aiden forget, for the briefest of moments, what exactly he was supposed to be doing.

He inhaled sharply, instantly aware of exactly how long he had been without a willing lass beneath him. Not that she was willing, nor was this the right time to pursue such an endeavor. Yet he could not resist the impulse to lean down and put his nose into her hair and breathe deeply.

But a gasp of outrage and a well-placed elbow into his stomach caused Aiden to ponder his sanity yet again. Exactly who was this woman?

# CHAPTER 3

*J*ona's chest heaved in outrage that she was being held thusly. How dare this beast of a man handle her in such a way? Just wait until her husband learned of this! She still held the knife in her hand but that did not last for long, for her assailant grabbed her wrist and squeezed. Her fingers instantly became numb, the blade falling uselessly to the floor. At least she had made her one opportunity count. She could only pray the cut she had inflicted caused enough damage, wherever the blade had managed to reach.

Worried for her wellbeing, she began to struggle. The only outcome was to be pulled firmly across a firm chest that surely must be carved from solid granite. The more she attempted to wiggle herself free, the tighter he held her. Who was this man and how had he managed to escape the guard's notice?

"Unhand me, ye fiend," she hissed angrily. Was that a muffled laugh she heard behind her?

"I highly doubt you can be trusted with your freedom,

lassie," the man answered, and Iona detected a hint of humor in his voice. But there could also be no mistaking the slight Scottish brogue in the tone of his voice. *A Scotsman attacking Dunborough?* That did not make any sense whatsoever.

"Ye have my word," Iona answered. Already she was thinking of the many ways she could escape his presence to go and find her husband. Surely there was no sin in lying when you were protecting yourself from possible physical harm.

"You must think I am a fool if you believe I would take you at your word that you would not attempt to escape me," her captor said with a snide laugh.

She shrugged, although confused for now the man sounded more English than Scot. "Who am I tae call ye a fool? Mayhap ye are, if ye are attempting tae seize something that does not belong tae ye." She was spun around so quickly, her breath rushed from her lungs. If she thought having her back to this man was troubling, 'twas nothing compared to having her heaving breasts within close proximity of his muscled torso. She watched in morbid curiosity as his head inched downward as if to place a kiss upon her startled lips. "Nay," she mumbled attempting to bring her hands up to push him away.

He halted his movement as if he realized his intent. "Perchance another time, fair maiden," he declared with a chuckle.

Before she knew what was happening, she was shoved, none too gently, into a chair. Faster than she thought possible, he pulled at her bed coverings. Taking a dirk from his belt, he tore the linen into strips and tied her to the chair.

"How dare ye! Release me at once," Iona demanded, whilst continuing to struggle to loosen the bindings at her wrists and ankles.

"I think not. No sense alerting all and sundry as to what is going on here."

"Just who do ye think ye are?" Was it just her imagination or did the remainder of the glowing embers in the hearth cause her captor's eyes to eerily glow as if he was possessed by the devil himself?

He smiled, causing Iona to swallow hard. "Why, I am your new master, of course."

"I have no master," she cried out angrily.

The man before her laughed. "We shall see…"

Before she could give another nasty retort, he came to her with the last of the linen. A wicked gleam entered his eyes before he placed a brief kiss upon her lips before he gagged her. She squirmed in protest.

"Perchance one day we will look back on this brief encounter and remind ourselves that our relationship began with a kiss," he murmured into her ear before he stepped back to study her intently. In disbelief, she then watched him give her a jaunty bow before leaving her room.

Iona silently vowed he would pay for what he had done to her once she gained her freedom. Even as she wiggled her hands and fingers in an attempted to loosen the bindings and reach for the knife she kept hidden in her boots, the door opened silently, and her son snuck into the room to come to her aid.

# CHAPTER 4

*B*roden Ferguson could barely hide his contempt for his brother who stood before him. He was tired of acting the carefree and sometimes ridiculous fool his older brother thought him to be. Being a younger son had never sat well with Broden and when Ewan had taken over as laird of Dunborough, Broden's life had gone from bad to worse.

Even Iona had betrayed him by choosing to be the lady of the keep rather than married to a landless younger son. *She should have been mine,* he thought, never mind that she had never shown even a remote inclination to favor his suit. And then, when she had given Ewan a son, his situation was doomed. Gregor's birth ensured that inheriting the estate would never be within Broden's grasp. His hatred for his brother was getting harder and harder to conceal. He was not sure why he even bothered any more.

"'Tis true then?" Ewan demanded, his hand on the hilt of his sword. "Ye went against my wishes to steal cattle from the McDowells?"

Broden gave a merry laugh. "'Twas a bet amongst the men that I could do it. Ye know I could not resist such a wager. Do ye not remember the days in our youth when we would do such an act together just tae spite Da?"

"We are no longer young lads running around the countryside at our whim and able tae be so reckless, brother. When will ye grow up and realize that the clan and its people must needs always come first?"

Broden gave a wave of his hand. "That is why ye are the laird and I am but yer most humble servant," he bowed mockingly.

"Do ye never take life seriously, brother?" Ewan asked.

Broden rolled his eyes. "Why should I? Life is short and there is plenty of ale tae drink and women tae make happy." Broden strode across the room and plopped himself down into a chair. Lifting his legs, his boots banged upon the table containing parchment most likely relating to the estate. He held back another chuckle but was amused when Ewan lifted his brows at his audacity, not that Broden took his feet off the table to appease the man.

"Ye should leave the village lasses alone before ye either get another one pregnant or find yerself at the end of a blade for messing with a lass who is wed," Ewan commanded. "My coffers are still not filled from the mess I needed tae clean up for ye from the last married lass ye violated. Her husband still complains about the bairn ye put in her belly."

"Ye worry too much and 'twas not my babe. This is what happens when I moved my things into the village tae live instead of residing inside the castle."

"No one told ye tae move yer things from Dunborough," Ewan stated, whilst staring upon him.

"What else was I to do once ye married? Ye took the best of the lot that our humble little village had tae offer. Why, I may need tae go all the way tae Edinburgh before I find another I might fancy." He realized his mistake, as did his brother, whose gaze narrowed into a fierce frown.

"*God's wounds!* Tell me I am mistaken and ye do not covet my wife?" Ewan bellowed, his face turning purple with uncontained anger.

Tired of constantly hiding his true self, he blurted out everything he had been holding inside for years. "It took ye long enough tae figure it out. What she sees in ye is beyond my ken, but one day ye shall meet an early demise. I look forward tae the day, so I can at last claim her as my own," he smirked with a slight chuckle. His brother could be so very dense at times.

Ewan staggered back. "Iona was right about ye but ye shall never have her. I shall kill ye myself before I let that occur."

Broden picked up a dirk and slipped it into his belt. "Empty threats, brother. Ye could no more kill me than ye could kill an enemy at our gates."

"Then I shall take Iona and Gregor and leave these lands if that means she and my son will be safe from ye. Clearly, family means nothing tae ye."

"Aye, ye have that aright. When it comes tae getting what I want, I plan on taking it no matter the cost. Besides, ye and I both know ye would never leave here, not when the clan needs ye."

"The devil take ye, Broden," Ewan swore.

Before Broden could comment further, the tower bell resounded a warning to the inhabitants that danger was near.

"The call to arms," Ewan cried out, taking up his sword. "It should not be too difficult for ye tae fight for the castle, given this is the land of yer birth."

"Damn ye to hell, Ewan," Broden mumbled beneath his breath. He pulled forth his sword and began heading toward the door.

Broden followed his brother into the dimly lit passageway. Clearly the battle had already begun, since the sound of shouting knights was heard in the night air. But what drew Broden to a halt was hearing the distinct sound of chainmail *ching chinging* its way down the passageway. The noise began to grow closer and he knew it was only a matter of seconds before they would be set upon.

With an evil grin, Broden pulled his sword forward and pushed the blade into Ewan's back. A coward's move perchance, but one that met his objective of having his brother finally out of the way. He jerked the blade out just as quickly, ensuring his brother would bleed out in no time.

Ewan fell to his knees with a groan of despair before pitching forward. His sword skittered across the stones. "Bro—den… help me," he wheezed, before he managing to turn over to stare with stunned eyes at what his brother had done. A pool of blood began seeping from his still body.

"Ye can help me by dying," Broden sneered before he wiped his blade on his brother's tunic.

He listened whilst his brother took his last dying breath and then put his unexpected plan into action. "Help! He has murdered our laird," Broden yelled, knowing that he would be heard and one of the invading forces would be held accountable for Ewan's death. With the enemy fast approaching, Broden took off in the opposite direction to find the garrison knights to help protect him. He never once looked back nor felt even the least bit of remorse for what he had done to his own kin.

Iona raced along the passageway with a firm grasp on Gregor's hand. She had to find Ewan and possibly escape the castle to the safety in her old home in the village. The sounds of knights in battle should have told her to find a chamber and bolt the door, yet how could she remain hidden when her captor could return at any moment?

A voice echoed off the walls and she prayed she was mistaken when she had heard that someone had killed Ewan. She ran faster, all but dragging her son with her. She rounded a corner of the passageway but came to a skidding halt. The unknown man who had tied her up was leaning over the body of someone on the cold stone floor. But she would recognize her husband anywhere.

"Nay!"

"Papa," Gregor yelled, pulling himself from her arms and running toward his father.

Iona did not think. She pulled the dirk from her boot and ran at the man who had killed Ewan. Slashing her arm forward, she managed to nick the man's face before he was once more grabbing her arm, causing the knife to fall. The sound of Gregor's sobs filled the passageway.

"Let me go! 'Tis my husband ye have killed, ye merciless

bastard," she screamed, whilst plummeting her fists on his chest. It damaged her own hands more than it did him, as the links of his chainmail dug into her flesh.

"I did not kill him, lass."

"Liar!"

The sound of more knights coming down the corridor caused the man before her to shove Gregor in her direction. "Get the lad out of here. 'Tis no place for a woman and a wee lad to be found."

"Ye shall pay and pay dearly for what ye have done this night. I vow if 'tis the last thing I do, ye shall pay for what ye have taken from me."

With a shake of her fist, she grabbed her son's hand. "Come, Gregor. There is nothing we can do for yer papa now."

"We canna leave him here, mama," he whimpered.

"Aye, we have no choice. I willna lose ye both in one night."

She gave one last look at her husband before she ran from the sight that would surely haunt her for many months to come.

# CHAPTER 5

$\mathcal{A}$iden stared into the angry eyes of the man he was told was Broden Ferguson, younger brother to the laird of the keep. There was still too much chaos at the moment to determine if the laird was in hiding or had been killed during the siege. But this man had raised his sword toward Aiden, giving him several slashes on his body. For this reason alone, the man needed to be punished.

The Scot's hands were bound and he was kneeling before Aiden, and was none too happy with his current predicament. Aiden was certain that, given the choice, Broden would rather try to run him through with his sword again than kneel there suffering at Aiden's feet. The man's eye was turning a nasty shade of purple whilst blood ran from a cut at his temple and a corner of his lip. He had put up quite the fight and Aiden could appreciate the knight's duty to protect his kinsmen.

The taking of the keep had not gone completely as planned but 'twas at least now under his control. Luckily, the bloodshed that had occurred had been minimal but 'twas still a loss in Aiden's mind. He would need to assess who in the household had been lost and what their purpose was in maintaining the estate. He would not mind also finding out who was the hellion who escaped from her chamber. Obviously, she had been married, but unfortunately that was no longer the case.

"Ye willna get away with this," Broden sneered.

"It appears you are wrong, since I have indeed already laid ownership to this land."

"The king will send men tae reclaim what is his."

Aiden lifted one brow. The man had courage to speak his mind, he would give him that much. "King Henry II of England most assuredly will know I have not failed in my quest to win him this stronghold."

Broden spat in the direction of Aiden's boots, a knowing jeer marring his bruised face. "Bah! Yer English pig is no king o' mine."

Aiden suppressed his own knowing grin. "We shall see. Throw him into a dungeon cell, if one can be found. If he gives you any problems, see if there is a pit to cease his arguments, where he can learn some manners."

A roar of outrage erupted from Broden, followed by curses damning Aiden to hell. It took two knights to force the man from the great hall. Aiden flicked his fingers towards one of his men he had fought beside.

"I can see you scowling at me, Finlay. You may as well speak your mind," Aiden stated, as he picked up a chalice of wine and motioned for his comrade to take a seat next to him.

Finlay lowered himself into the chair with a heavy sigh. "I

am having a strange sense of having been through this situation before. I like it not."

Aiden peered at him over the rim of his cup. Taking a large gulp, he set it down. "'Tis nothing out of the ordinary. I was asked by our king to take this land in his name. I have done so and now will reap the benefits of my victory."

"Such an action will not make it right in the eyes of the people you will now rule in his name. 'Tis not like Berwyck, being located right on the borders of two countries. We are too far north," Finlay replied. He reached for a piece of venison on a platter before them, bit into the meat and then wiped the juice from his lips upon his sleeve.

"They will learn to obey me," Aiden replied with confidence. "They have little choice in the matter. What's done is done."

"And yet, this is exactly the very same type of situation that caused ye tae leave Berwyck in the first place. How is what ye are doing any different than what yer brother-in-law Dristan did when he lay siege tae Berwyck Castle taking over yer homeland and inheritance?"

A moment of bitterness leaped into Aiden's mind as regret for those who lost their lives in the battle filled him with grief. "You are leaning dangerously close to incurring my wrath. Leave it be, Finlay."

"If ye do not hear this from me, then who else will ye hear it from?" Finlay asked, leaning back into his chair. "I have been a part of the MacLaren clan with ye and yer sister Amiria for as long as I can remember. I watched whilst she buried yer father and mourned for the loss of her twin because she thought ye were among the dead. Since ye were whisked off during the battle tae recover from yer injuries, ye were not there tae see the utter destruction and turmoil that battle caused yer family and the clan."

"You know nothing of what I have been through," Aiden muttered, taking another sip of his wine. "How dare you question my motives? I would think you, of all people, would understand my need to prove myself and earn the respect of a king who can award me lands and monies if I but do his bidding."

"At what cost, Aiden? Is taking this castle really going tae get ye the respect of the very people ye have just conquered?"

"Only time will tell the outcome," Aiden answered swallowing hard the bitterness that leapt into his throat.

"Ye are far beyond the English borders, my friend. I would think yer Scottish heritage would be warring within itself."

"Leave off, Finlay."

They sat in silence, both lost in thought. The only sound was the fire crackling in the hearth. All else was eerily silent, as though the castle itself was a shadow of a ghost. Finlay's words hit far closer to the truth of the matter than Aiden cared to admit, even to himself.

"What of the woman?" Finlay finally asked.

"What woman?"

"Let us not play games, my friend. Ye and I both know which woman I speak of. It cannot sit well that ye killed her husband."

A low growl erupted from Aiden. "I did not kill him. Someone stabbed the man in the back. I never could stand a coward, but he did not die by my blade, I swear it."

"Again... 'tis a situation that is too common tae the happenings at Berwyck, only instead of a father dying 'tis someone's husband."

"'Tis always someone's husband or brother. People die in war, and such cannot be helped."

Finlay clucked his tongue. "Well… no matter the cause, she will hate ye for it."

Aiden looked up. "Have you found her as yet?"

"Nay. If she is still somewhere inside the castle, then she is hiding herself well."

Aiden nodded finishing off his wine. "I am certain she will turn up. If nothing else, she will wish to see that her husband is given a proper burial. Make arrangements for the people to claim their kin so they may be buried. We must needs also find a priest who will bless the graves."

As Aiden watched Finlay leave to fulfill the orders he was given, he looked around the empty hall as his friend's words echoed inside his head. God above, he hoped all his efforts would be worth it.

# CHAPTER 6

*I*ona stood at Ewan's gravesite, tears streaming down her face. Her son was oddly silent, given he had just lost his father. The priest's words, as he droned on in prayer, barely reached her numb mind. In one heartbeat, her life had changed. Now that Ewan was gone, how was she to support her son? Her small farm had barely made enough for her to survive prior to her marriage, let alone to sell goods to see them through the coming winter. Her fields were fallow, for the land had not been worked to provide for the coming winter. Now she needed to support herself and Gregor, and with no husband.

That her brother-in-law was not in attendance at Ewan's burial bothered her only somewhat. The two men had never been close, and she had no idea what Broden's fate had been when their home had been overcome by their enemy. Did he yet live or did he perchance also die in the heat of battle during a siege that was over before most knew it had even begun? She only knew that, if he were dead, she would no longer have to worry about his obscene advances whenever Ewan was nowhere in sight. She shivered at the thought of his touch.

The sound of those around her saying *amen* brought Iona out of the musings. She walked closer to the grave and took up a handful of dirt. She scrunched the soil into the palm of her hand before tossing it into the grave. She stood by silently and watched as the gesture was repeated by those who had known her husband. Two men who were her neighbors came and began shoveling the dirt into Ewan's grave while the priest moved on to the next burial site. Iona did everything in her power not to break down in front of her son.

"What will become of us now, mama?" Gregor's small voice echoed Iona's own thoughts. That a boy of only nine summers should be worrying over his fate did not seem fair. She took a deep breath to steady her nerves.

"We shall take things one day at a time, son. Do not fret. I will think of something." She reached out to ruffle his dark hair, so much like Ewan's that her heart ached. She heard her son's name being called by a few of the other local lads. Iona did not have to wait for Gregor to ask if he could join them. He might as well find whatever happiness he could. "Go on. Be home for supper."

Gregor handed her a flower he had been holding and did not wait to see if she would change her mind. He ran to join his friends. At least for a while he could be a carefree lad once more.

Once Ewan's grave was filled, the men gave her a nod before moving on to the next one. Iona went to kneel beside it and placed the flower Gregor had given her below the crude wooden cross with her husband's name etched upon it. Caressing the lettering, she began to cry in earnest, now that she was alone, and she hid her face in the palms of her hands. Despair all but consumed her whilst she pondered how on this earth she would survive.

A whisper on the wind sounded as though it carried her name, giving her pause in her grief at losing her husband. She gazed around almost in the hopes of seeing Ewan coming towards her. Tears of grief turned sharply to tears of anger at who was drawing near.

Now that she could see this man in the light of day, she almost choked that someone she vowed to hate could be so handsome. Hair as red as her own framed a chiseled visage that surely must be carved from granite, much like the chest that she had been molded against the night before. A black cape hung from broad shoulders and billowed behind him from the ocean breeze. A sword swung from a scabbard that was belted at his lean hips and she cursed herself for taking a moment to appreciate the fine-looking man that he was. He appeared no older than herself and yet the way he carried himself made him seem much older.

Iona looked away and was startled to realize that her heart was racing the closer this stranger came. Considering what this man had cost her, she had to find it in herself to guard against such an immediate attraction.

A hand was thrust in front of her face, and she slapped away his offer to help her rise. She did so instead, on her own. Raising her head, she put on what she hoped was a calm face but resolve slipped when she stared into the most amazing violet eyes she had ever seen before. *Violet? Really? God's wounds, how could this man have eyes the shade of the heather on the Scottish moors?*

His hand fell to his side as he made her a short bow. "Madam, I am sorry for your loss," he said reverently.

If Iona had not known better, then she might believe his words of condolences. "I somehow doubt the person responsible for my husband's death would care tae offer me solace."

"I am not responsible for his death, my lady."

"I am no lady, nor am I yers," she answered with a bitter laugh at life's irony. With the taking of the keep, she was no longer Dunborough's mistress and had been reduced to nothing more than a village lass once more.

His face seemingly portrayed remorse but how could she ever trust him? He continued as if she hadn't interrupted him. "I repeat, I told you I had nothing to do with your husband's death, in case you have forgotten."

"I forget nothing! How do ye think I can erase the image of seeing ye hovering over my dead husband's body?" she snapped.

He gave a heavy sigh. "Sometimes all that you see is not necessarily as it appears. Just because I was near his body does not mean I killed the man. I came here determined to avoid bloodshed."

"Ye should not be here at all! Go back tae England where ye belong," she bellowed.

"This is my home now. You best resign yourself to the fact that I now shall rule this land in the name of King Henry II."

"An English King's man on Scottish soil? Ye shall be lucky if ye live tae see the se'nnight out."

"Are you threatening me?"

"Ha! I do not need tae threaten ye, my laird. Those who shall take up arms in the name of King William shall dispose of ye and yer men who defile this land with yer presence."

The man before her ran his fingers through his hair. "We are off to a bad start. Let us begin again. I am Aiden of Clan MacLaren, originally of Berwyck to the south, and you are..." his voice trailed away as Iona continued to stare in disbelief at his words. Did he honestly think she would accept him as a friend?

Her lips snapped shut before she could finally form any sort of words to answer him. "What, in all that is holy, makes ye believe that I would give a damn on who ye are, let alone from whence ye hail?"

"I am trying to make amends for the rift between us. Surely you can understand that I will need all my people to help maintain the land surrounding the castle," Aiden replied as he continued to stare upon her.

"We are *not* yer people."

"Aye, you are and as such I offer you and everyone in the village my protection."

Iona could not hold back her mirth. "Yer protection? Surely ye must jest! Ye offer such a service after ye have killed how many knights in yer greed to steal land that does not belong tae ye?"

Iona began pacing back and forth, wondering what Aiden of Berwyck could possibly want from her but she saw the way his eyes watched her and supposed 'twas not that hard to figure out, the cad. "Begone with ye," she threatened, "and leave us in peace tae mourn our dead. We need not some English lord bragging tae all who shall listen how he is now the conquering hero."

She left him standing there as she went to catch up with the rest of the villagers who were already listening to the priest bless the next grave. Before long the lonely sounds of a bagpipe sounded out to help the dead pass on to the afterlife and also to give whatever solace they could find to those who were left behind to mourn.

# CHAPTER 7

*A*iden watched the woman leave still not even knowing her name. The grave she had mourned over offered no clues to who this woman was. She said she was no lady and yet she had been found in a chamber inside the castle walls. Who was she? Her identity continued to plague his mind, but he would let the matter rest for now. He was here to show support to those who had lost their loved ones. Every loss mattered to Aiden. He honestly did not want even one person to die in his quest to win the castle without unnecessary violence.

"'Twas inevitable that there would be bloodshed," Finlay reminded him, as though the man had read his mind.

"Aye, I know, but still… how am I to win these people over and gain their respect if I am seen as their enemy?" Aiden asked, as he and his men moved on to the next grave.

"Perchance with enough time…" Finlay answered as he looked ahead toward the other graves.

Giving a silent prayer, Aiden looked over at the rest of his men who had followed him into this mess with no questions asked. Finlay had been with his sister's personal guard. The oldest of the group, he had no issue when Aiden asked if he would join him on his quest for fame and fortune. Colin and Duncan swore their allegiance to him and would not be left behind at Berwyck. Since they, too, were unwed, they had their own selfish reasons for leaving the MacLaren clan behind. This left Logan who had joined him after a tournament in France. All Scotsman at heart and only wanting to be back in the land of their birth.

*Land of their birth...* Aiden heaved a sigh, thinking his own heritage was a jumbled mess. Raised by a Scottish Laird who had married an Englishwoman, his own memories warred within him that his actions last eve were doing one of his parents wrong. Did they even now look down upon him from the heavens and worry over his choices to do all he could for an English king? He had fond memories of his mother, what he could remember of her since she died giving birth to the youngest MacLaren, Patrick. She had taken extra care with her children's upbringing, unusual for the lady of a keep. 'Twas only natural that his accent, along with those of his siblings, would sound more English than Scottish, the latter only becoming pronounced when they became angry or agitated.

He knew the task ahead of him would be daunting, but he was never one to back down from a challenge. The taking of the keep in the name of King Henry was only one step toward having the status that had been his at the time of his birth.

There had been a brief time of bitterness knowing he had lost Berwyck Castle to the champion knight of the very English king Aiden now claimed to serve. Irony… 'twas going to eat him alive if he dwelled on the matter. But his sister was happy with her husband and at least she was now lady of their home and of Clan MacLaren.

"God's Blood, but that is a fine bonny lass," Colin proclaimed as he stared at a woman in the distance.

"Aye… I have seen several who I would like tae see might favor my suit," Logan chimed in, rubbing the back of his neck. "If only 'twere that simple."

Duncan laughed, causing several people nearby to frown. "They shall never see us in any other light than the conquering foe so ye best look elsewhere for yer wives!"

Aiden's gaze traveled to the red-haired beauty who continued to keep his attention. She was a fiery one, that was for sure, and he would not mind getting to know her. "Mayhap with time… as Finlay suggested."

"We could be waiting for the second coming and I still do not think 'twill be enough time for such a miracle tae occur, my friends," grumbled Finlay. "Perchance we should just head back home tae Berwyck."

Aiden was startled by his friend's reply and shook his head. "You all, of course, are welcome to come and go as you see fit. As for me… well… I am now home."

Silence filled the group as each man decided his own fate. Aiden held his breath hoping his friends would remain as loyal to him as they had since they left Berwyck's gates many years ago.

"Ye know I shall stay by yer side, Aiden," Finlay replied placing his hand upon Aiden's shoulder.

"As will I," Logan chimed in.

"Aye!" Duncan and Colin said in unison as they also placed their hands in the circle around Aiden that had been formed. A sign of camaraderie along with years of friendship that apparently would remain unbroken. Aiden would not take their sacrifice on his behalf lightly.

"You honor me with your vows to stay with me," Aiden humbly replied with a sincere heart. "I know what you are giving up by continuing to serve me along with the other knights that even now guard the castle walls."

"We have not lifted our swords with ye all these years to give up on ye now, Aiden," Finlay said with a final pat on Aiden's back.

Logan gave a low laugh. "Well, if we are all now done being overly melodramatic with our brotherly bond, mayhap we should continue our vigil at these graves for a show of support to the villagers."

"Aye," Duncan nodded. "I think we should be done with this public display of affection for one another before the locals think us all daft."

The group of men gave a low laugh and began making their way ahead. Aiden lingered in thought as he espied the boy who had summoned the alarm last night. He waved the lad over. He seemed reluctant to leave his friends, but finally began making his way toward Aiden whilst he heaved his shoulders back as though he carried the weight of the world on those small shoulders.

Dark brown hair and eyes just as brown filled with hatred stared up at Aiden. The boy was surely not more than ten summers whilst he jutted out his chin in such defiance that Aiden held back a laugh. A lad making every attempt at being a full-grown man. He fell short but Aiden gave him the credit he deserved for showing no fear in the face of what the boy would consider the enemy.

"What is your name, boy?" Aiden asked folding his arms across his chest.

The boy copied his gesture. "Why do ye wish tae know my name?"

"How else am I to address my subjects if I do not know what to call them?" Aiden responded with authority.

The boy pondered Aiden's response before he finally answered. "I suppose it canna hurt for ye to know it."

Aiden waited for the boy's answer and when none came, he gently prodded the lad. "And are you planning on giving it to me or do we stand here all day?"

"I thought making ye wait might be good for ye," the boy said before laughing in childish delight.

Aiden's brow lifted at the boy's nerve to defy him. "You are a brave one, you are. First you watch me climb a cliff in amusement and then you run to alert the night watch. You will make a fine knight one day."

The boy puffed out his chest at the compliment. "I will be better than you because I will not get caught when I take siege of a keep!"

Aiden threw back his head and gave a hearty laugh. "I will look forward to hearing of your tales of your quests as I feel there will be many. Now, young lad… your name."

"'Tis Gregor," the boy answered.

"And I am Aiden of Clan MacLaren but now calling Dunborough my home."

"Ye be Scottish?"

"And English but that is another story. What is your surname, young Gregor."

He hesitated before finally answering him with tear-filled eyes. A startling contrast to the confident lad that disappeared into a grieving youth. "Ferguson," Gregor whispered.

And that was the moment that Aiden realized that the young boy standing before him would have stood to inherit the estate that Aiden now claimed. A sense of *déjà vu* filled Aiden with regret whilst his past collided with his future. 'Twas as though everything in his life was repeating itself now that Aiden had stolen this boy's future.

"Your father?" Aiden asked, already knowing the answer.

"Over there," Gregor pointed to the grave where he had seen the lady he was curious about grieving.

"And your mother? Who is she?" Aiden inquired.

Gregor looked around until he saw his mother and pointed to the red-haired beauty. "My mother is Lady Iona Ferguson, lately of the hall ye now call yer home, I suppose."

Aiden nodded and noticed the lady had finished her prayers at the grave. She saw Aiden having speech with her son and began storming her way toward them. He did not have long to wait before she erupted in full anger.

"Keep away from my son!" she fumed pulling Gregor into her arms.

"Mama, let me go," Gregor cried out in what Aiden assumed was embarrassment that he was being coddled.

"Go and join your friends tae play for a wee bit," she ordered the boy, "and then return home tae the cottage. I shall have supper waiting for ye."

Aiden waited for the boy to leave before giving the woman a proper bow. "Lady Iona…"

She placed her hands on her hips. "I presume my son gave up my name."

"Aye. Reluctantly if that makes a difference to you."

"I suppose 'twas only a matter of time before ye found out," she replied.

"Is there a reason you did not wish for me to know you were the lady of the hall?" Aiden asked placing his hands behind his back. Her blue eyes widened before she answered him.

"I am no longer the lady of the hall as of last night and yer taking of the keep. I would, however, appreciate the courtesy of time tae retrieve my things from my bedchamber so I can have them removed and taken tae my cottage in the village."

Aiden shook his head. "There is no need to move." Her startled expression told him much and he probably should have thought what his words might mean to her.

A gasp escaped her lips. "Ye think tae keep me as some plaything tae use at yer leisure?" she cried out. "Ye are mistaken, sir, if ye think that I am part of what ye feel ye have taken!"

"I meant no disrespect, nor did I wish to imply you were part of the… victory I have earned."

"I am no man's plaything tae do with as ye will," she fumed.

"And again… I did not mean to imply you were such. Although anyone with any sense can see you are a treasure beyond compare," Aiden said quietly and watch a blush cross her features.

Her mouth opened and closed several times, giving him the impression she was at a loss for words. He held back a grin. *Mayhap this is a beginning between us.*

"I still wish tae gather my things," she said with a toss of her head. He watched in fascination as those red tresses seemed to come alive as they fell back into place.

"A discussion we can have on the morrow... if you would but indulge me, that is," Aiden said softly. "Mayhap at the afternoon meal?"

She pondered him for a moment before she nodded her head. "I suppose it couldna hurt tae have speech then tae discuss the matter."

"Then I shall indeed look forward to the morrow, my lady," Aiden replied with a small smile.

"Until the morrow..." Iona answered before taking her leave.

Aiden watched her depart again, her swaying hips tempting him further in his fascination with the beautiful Iona. God help him if he ever gave his heart to the woman!

# CHAPTER 8

*I*ona left her small cottage and began making her way toward the castle. Each step she took weighed deeply on her mind. The problem of caring for Gregor on her own was a heavy burden that left Iona feeling completely alone with no one to turn to for aid. When she was being honest with herself, she wasn't sure she could manage. Also weighing on her mind was the way the villagers looked at her. They had grown used to thinking of her as the lady of the keep and now they treated her as if she did not know her place. In her mind, she had stepped from an important position within the clan back to nothing more than one of the lasses in the village. 'Twas a problem for sure. She was certain she would never fit in amongst them again as she did before her marriage to Ewan.

*Ewan...* her steps faltered and a sob wretched itself from the depths of her soul. Her gentle giant lay in the cold ground, killed at the hands of the very enemy she was about to meet with. How would she manage? She was still unclear why she had agreed to such an engagement in the first place.

The new laird swore he had not killed her husband. If his words were true, then the question remained of who had done such a dastardly deed. No man of worth would kill a man from behind. The memory of seeing Aiden yesterday filled her head and her heart began to beat furiously in her chest.

'Twas those damn violet eyes of his that had been her undoing, or perchance 'twas more. She had never had such instant feelings for a man before. How was she going to control her emotions in front of the man? He was her enemy, was he not? Confusion warred with the anger she should be feeling toward Aiden MacLaren, yet a small part of her yearned for what had been missing from her life. What was she thinking to allow such feelings into her heart for the very man she should hate?

A slight breeze traveled from the ocean and seemingly wrapped itself around her making her cape float behind her as if she was about to take flight. She closed her eyes to listen to a soft murmur that was so reminiscent of her husband she found comfort in the sound. 'Twas as though he stood right before her, wrapping those strong arms around her to give her strength for what was to come. She gave a contented sigh, gratified with the feeling he was near but still knowing 'twas impossible.

Opening her eyes revealed nothing but the path ahead of her and her disappointment knew no bounds. Ewan was gone from her life forever. She had loved him to the best of her ability, but she had never been *in* love with him and maybe this was the reason for the anger that rose within her. She should have loved him in her heart. Yet one look at the conquering hero that now took up residence in what was once her home caused her heart to flutter madly in her chest. Would she be ready to proclaim her undying love for this man next? Iona scoffed at the idea. The thought was not only ludicrous but downright wrong. She refused to think she could give her heart away to this man so easily.

She continued her way through the village, nodding to several people who stopped what they were doing to either bow or curtsey to her, calling her milady. She nodded in return, plastering a smile upon her face, but inwardly she once more sighed. Going back to being one of them was going to be harder than she thought.

She came upon the small spit of ground separating the mainland from the seaside cliff that Dunborough was perched. Two unfamiliar knights stood guard when she approached one of two gates. She waved to the men above the barbican gate and they allowed her to pass. 'Twas obvious they knew she was expected, and she began to wonder what other changes had occurred in her brief absence.

Iona did not have to ponder her question for long, since the answer was apparent once she came through the gate into the inner bailey. Another two guards came to escort her to the keep and one pounded on the metal door to seek entrance. Once she entered, there were more knights on the other side; one she remembered seeing but yesterday with the new laird. He bowed before her, and she took notice of his tawny-colored hair and green eyes. Who was this man and why did it seem that all the men accompanying the new laird were just as handsome?

"Lady Iona," his deep rich Scottish accent hinted at his origin, "I am Finlay, lately of Berwyck. I have been asked tae escort ye tae Laird Aiden." He held out his arm as any knight with manners would do but Iona was reluctant to reach for his offering.

Indecision overwhelmed her. "I am certain I can make my way on my own, good sir."

A chuckle escaped him. "I have no doubt of that, my lady, but indulge me on my attempt tae put ye at ease."

"Put me at ease? Are ye jesting with me? How in heaven's name above could ye possibly put me at ease with anything that is going on in my life?" she asked waving her hand toward the castle interior.

"'Tis but a simple offering, my lady, with no disrespect intended." He continued to hold his arm out waiting for her decision.

She silently cursed, knowing she was probably appearing scattered and irrational, not that she cared what this invader thought of her. She at last put her hand on his extended arm.

"Very well," she managed to say through clenched teeth. "Lead the way."

Iona kept her eyes straight ahead, although she took note that not all that much had changed since she last walked the grounds of her home... his home now. The knights above on the parapet may be different than Ewan's men but they still guarded the castle just as vigilantly as those who had come before them.

They entered the foyer through the main door and she tried not to get emotional when she glanced into the empty great hall. She would have found it hard to see someone other than her husband and herself sitting on the raised dais or the main chairs set before the hearth. 'Twas clear her audience with the new laird was not to happen in her hall. So where was she meeting him?

Finlay continued to escort her through the foyer until they reached the turret stairs. Upon reaching the fourth floor, Iona stumbled to a halt. There were only so many rooms on this floor that always belonged to the laird and lady of the keep. Surely, she would not be brought to Aiden's bedchamber.

"Where exactly are you taking me?" she asked in a hushed tone.

"Tae Laird Aiden's solar, my lady, have no fear," Finlay replied, as he began to again walk down the passageway.

The solar… thank heavens her first assumption would not come to pass. Still, when they passed what used to be her bedchamber and then Ewan's, her breath leapt into her throat until they reached the solar door. It opened to reveal Aiden sitting behind Ewan's desk. The castle steward, Seumas, was by his side whilst they perused the ledgers. To not see her own departed husband behind the desk that portrayed the importance of laird was more of a shock than she expected. Her knees buckled and Finlay grabbed her waist before she fell to the floor.

She was unsure how Aiden moved so quickly to reach her side, only that he scooped her up into his arms and carried her across the room to sit in the very chair she had occupied for many years. In fact, she glanced down to see the bit of sewing she had been working on in a basket. He carefully set her down in her chair and a cry left her at the injustice of her life. She buried her face in her hands until hers were taken into Aiden's warm ones. Violet eyes filled with concern for her welfare stared down upon her and confused emotions ran amuck inside her head. The heat of his body next to hers as he knelt by the chair was going to be her undoing.

"Wine!" Aiden called out. A chalice was thrust into his waiting palm, and he placed the cup near her lips. "Drink."

She continued to stare into those hypnotizing eyes until her shaking hands palmed the cup and she did as she was told. The wine slid down her throat and calmed her until she pushed the chalice away. Aiden took it from her and set it down on a table that was near, in case she wanted more.

"Better?" he asked quietly, taking her hand and rubbing his thumb over the back in a circular movement.

"Aye, thank ye," she managed to whisper, wondering what catastrophe would occur next. Nothing seemed simple anymore and she wondered where the strong woman she knew she was had disappeared to.

"Very well," Aiden said, before standing and going back to the desk. He shut the ledger and handed the book to Seumas. "I am impressed with your bookkeeping, and all appears in order. I would be pleased if you would continue on as steward, Seumas, if that is acceptable to you."

Seumas bowed. "As you wish, my laird."

"Good! Let us meet in another fortnight to go over the books again," Aiden replied with a nod of approval.

"Until then, my laird," Seumas said with another bow, before turning and repeating the gesture to Iona. "My lady."

An odd premonition fell over Iona at the irony of it all. She watched Seumas leave the room until Aiden turned to his knight. "Leave us, Finlay."

The knight frowned before his gazed fell upon her. "But, Aiden…"

"She is safe in my care, my friend. Leave us," Aiden ordered whilst Finlay snapped his mouth shut and reluctantly took his leave.

The room came to an eerie silence. Iona swallowed hard, not knowing what was to come next. She should not be alone in the room with this man... this man who could have lied to her when he proclaimed he did not kill her husband. How could she trust him? And yet when his eyes met hers, something in her shifted so suddenly she felt faint. Call it destiny... call it fate... whatever she called it, this insane emotion ran rampant through her heart. Something in her wanted so much to believe him and she did not know why!

She waited whilst he poured himself his own cup of wine and came to sit next to her in Ewan's chair. She supposed she must needs get used to the idea that the chair no longer belonged to her husband but to this handsome stranger who now silently stared back at her.

"You must be wondering why I asked for you to join me here today," Aiden said, taking a sip from his chalice before setting it down. He bent forward to rest his arms on his legs, bringing his body closer.

"Aye, yer... invitation, has crossed my mind a time or two since yesterday," Iona answered quietly. "What could we possibly discuss?"

"First... your living arrangements. I am certain you have come to learn that returning to your previous life will not work," Aiden began, folding his hands and continue to stare at her.

"Ye know nothing of my previous life," Iona snapped.

"I beg to differ."

"Ye should not presume—"

Aiden held up his hand to cut off the rest of her words. He then sat back in his chair, his elbows on the arms, his hands forming a steeple whilst he continued to assess her. "'Tis not hard to presume much where you are concerned, Lady Iona, and I have learned much of you and your family overnight," Aiden began, before he continued. "You were the lady of this hall, and your son Gregor is your only child. Your husband, Ewan Ferguson was laird of this very castle and was killed from behind..." he held up his hand again when she was about to give a nasty retort, "...and not by my own hand or that of any of my men, I will add. Your brother-in-law, Broden is even now sitting in a cell in the dungeon after being captured and taking out several of my men. He also made an attempt to kill me, which is why he is currently residing in the dungeon. His fate has yet to be determined, although I must admit I have never come across such an unpleasant person in my life."

"Ye have Broden in the dungeon?" she smirked in delight.

"You seem pleased he has been taken there."

"He deserves far worse, I assure ye," she answered smartly.

Aiden chuckled. "No love lost between the two of you, I see. Very well. He may just have earned an extended visit with the rats just to please you."

"Why should you care if his incarceration pleases me or not?" she asked with wide eyes.

"Let us just say that I wish for peace between us."

"Ye wish for peace but how is this possible when all will think of ye as the enemy?"

"That is where you come in, my lady."

"Me? What is it ye think I can do tae make yer transition tae laird more acceptable with the Ferguson clan and villagers?" She held her breath waiting for the answer, but she knew what he would say before he even uttered one word.

"With your help in showing the villagers you accept me as laird, of course." A slow smile crept across his lips, but Iona was leery of what exactly her help might entail.

"And what exactly do expect me tae do about it?" she asked with a frown.

"To begin with, you and your son will remain housed in your previous bedchambers as a sign that I have accepted you into my household as valued guests."

"Guests? If ye think tae keep me here against my wishes or as yer mistress, ye will be waiting for years tae come before I agree tae such an arrangement!"

Another chuckle rumbled in his chest. "I asked no such thing of you, Iona, but if we came to a certain... *agreement*... I promise you shall be happy in my bed."

A gasp of outrage left her. "Ye cad!"

"You are the one who brought up becoming my mistress and, whilst the idea does hold some appeal, I must decline at this time. You shall know if I am interested in pursuing such an arrangement when the situation is convenient for me and not before."

She abruptly stood; her face flushed in outrage. "How dare ye!"

"Sit back down, Iona," he ordered and waited until she complied.

"I willna be kept here against my will!" she fumed, before clenching her hands together. She had the notion she would rather claw the smug look off Aiden's face than to sit here calmly waiting for whatever he had in store for her next.

He ran his fingers through his red hair whilst several strands stood on end. He may not have known it but 'twas comical and he suddenly reminded her of a rooster. 'Twas most likely a fair assessment… a rooster after all the hens in the henhouse!

"If you would but let me finish, I will continue my proposal," Aiden said quietly with a raised brow as he waited for her answer.

"Go on…" Her words were skeptical, for she had no reason to believe anything he said nor to trust him.

He leaned forward again as if to prove the worth of his words. "You and your son will continue to dwell in the bedchambers you previously held whilst you were lady of this hall."

"Ye said that already. And if and when ye marry, what then?" she asked, knowing the man before her would be expected to wed and produce an heir.

"We shall worry about that when the time comes," Aiden replied.

"What else?"

"In return for my protection, you shall do your best to see me in a favorable light and share that view with the clan and villagers," he said sitting back in his chair.

"And just how do ye think I am tae perform such a miracle?" Ye willna be accepted so easily."

"Mayhap not, but with you by my side, perchance the task might not be too difficult to come to pass. All I ask is that you try."

"Try? My husband's murderer? Ye expect me tae stroll through the village on yer arm as though ye did not kill Ewan?"

His fist pounded on the arm of his chair. "I did not kill your husband for no knight with any sense of honor would kill another from behind! 'Tis the act of a coward. I swear to you I did not kill him!" he bellowed and for the first time, Iona was frightened of the man before her. He was unexpectedly in full battle mode, and she could see the knight behind the sword. Fierce. Unyielding. Determined to win the day...

Deep in her heart, Iona believed that this suddenly angry knight spoke the truth. She tried to form words to placate him. "Then who killed him?"

"I do not know but, if 'twill ease your suffering, I will also vow to find his killer. Can we find a common accord, my lady?" he asked, once more looking the carefree knight she had seen in the past few days.

She hesitated. How could she not? She was torn between her sense of commitment to her deceased husband and the possible answer to her problem of being able to provide for her son. Aiden seemed sincere when he offered her his protection and yet a portion of her still continued to be leery of his proposition. She would not become a kept woman!

"Ye offer myself and my son yer protection?" she inquired, knowing she had little choice but to accept this insane offer. 'Twas either this or starve. She had no resources to provide for herself and Gregor.

"I do."

"And ye promise ye willna expect me tae become yer mistress?" She held her breath waiting for his reply. A sly grin spread across his handsome features. God's Bones, but the man was beyond compare when he smiled at her like he was now doing. She was going to have a hard time of being in the same room with him let alone playing her part in the village.

"You have my word that nothing will happen between us unless you wish it, Iona." The husky baritone of his voice held a promise of what could happen between them. Iona refused to give in to him so easily, nor to herself!

"Very well. I accept yer offer but I swear tae ye that 'twill be a cold day in hell that I will ever willingly be found in yer bed!" She stood and turned to leave.

"Never say never, Iona." Aiden also stood and reached out for her hand. He brought her fingertips up to his lips. She waited to feel his mouth upon her now trembling skin but instead, he turned her hand upward and placed a kiss on the inside of her wrist. Her heart jumped into her throat and she wretched her hand from his.

She fled the solar, her quest to find her son and return to her cottage in the forefront of her mind. But as she ran down the passageways, she swore she could still feel Aiden's lips on her wrist. He would remain on her mind far into the evening hours.

# CHAPTER 9

*B*roden paced his cell like the caged animal he was. For nigh unto a fortnight, he had been left and forgotten in this hell hole. He supposed his fate could be worse. Dunborough's pit was a nasty and vile place, and he was thankful he had not been tossed down into those depths. Instead, he fought off the rats and mice whenever someone brought him food, if that is what it could be called. He closed his eyes and remembered the heavenly aroma of the great hall's evening meals. 'Twould be a long while before he would see such riches again unless he could be released from here.

He shivered in the cold dampness that was his prison. Captured when he killed one of the invading knights, he had fought off the rest, including their leader, to no avail. When brought before the last knight he had attempted to kill, he realized 'twas the new *laird*. Broden had spat at his feet.

The laird was after information, and none would be forthcoming from Broden. The fact someone had spilled his name irritated Broden. To think that he had been betrayed by another Ferguson! Broden certainly would not confess to killing his own brother and would not lose any sleep over the matter. Even if the situation had not turn out as he expected. Yet how was he to know that all he would gain by taking Ewan's life would be imprisonment? He pounded on the stone wall of his cell. *Bloody Hell*! All his plans were for naught. Instead of forcing Iona to wed him and becoming laird of the castle, he was now reduced to nothing more than a prisoner in a cell. He had to escape.

There were still a few men loyal to him above and Broden prayed they would be forming a plan for his release. He could then hide himself in the village until he could gather enough men to invade once more. He raised his fist heaven bound, swearing upon his life that he would one day become the rightful laird of this very castle!

As if his prayers had been heard, a light appeared in the passageway along with a familiar face that came to stand in front of his cell. Broden thrust his arms through the bars and grasped Angus's forearm.

"Ye came!" Broden said in relief. "Did ye find the key to the cell?"

Angus held up the brass key with a mighty laugh. "The daft Englishmen dinnae know what hit them when I offered them a drink with something in it tae make them sleep. About fell down the stairs when the drink took them."

"Get me the hell out of here then and let us make our way tae the village so ye can hide me there," Broden urged and as the lock clicked and the door swung open, he clapped his hands together in glee.

"Shouldna be that difficult tae keep tae the shadows of the night and make yer escape. Just dinnae get yerself caught. I dinnae go tae all this trouble for our plans tae go awry now," Angus muttered. He went inside the cell and shaped the extra blankets he carried to appear as though Broden were sleeping on the cot. He then left the cell and locked the door.

"Let us away," Broden exclaimed with a chuckle.

Up the stairs they went and as they reached the entryway, he stepped over the knights who were softly snoring. The stupid fools! Broden gave them no further thought as he made his way through a door leading outside. This was almost too easy, and he took extra care to keep to the shadows to not be seen.

Angus made a distraction at the rear postern gate, allowing Broden to open the door and make his escape across the narrow spit of land. The Englishman had already gotten lazy if Broden was able to escape this easily. He would be certain to use it against the new laird when he planned to overtake the keep.

# CHAPTER 10

$\mathcal{A}$iden kept a steady arm around Iona's waist as they made their way from the castle grounds over to the mainland, whilst several of his knights guarded their backs. He knew this narrow pathway was dangerous, but in the light of day it seemed even more so, as he saw that death awaited them if they put a single foot in the wrong place. They were striding on what could only be termed as the backbone of a narrow cliff, the ocean shore far below. A moment's negligence and they would meet their end. He had no intention of dying such an unseemly death, nor of allowing the lady or her son to do so.

Gregor's laughter rang out in the morning air as he picked up a rock and tossed it over the ledge. He went to the edge to peer down so he could watch it hit the cliffside and bounce into the ocean. "Are ye frightened, my laird?" the boy teasingly asked. He began walking backwards all the while watching Aiden behind mischievous brown eyes. The lad clearly took after his father, for there wasn't much resemblance to Iona that Aiden could see.

"Watch yer manners, Gregor," Iona warned as she, too, surveyed her steps.

"Mama... he knows I am but jesting. Besides, if he can climb the cliffside with nothing but the moon tae light his way, then this should be easy for him!"

Wide eyes turned to face Aiden. "Ye climbed the cliff?"

"It seemed the most sensible way to gain access to the castle in the dead of night," Aiden shrugged with a small smile.

"Ye could have easily died! 'Tis no small feat tae climb such deadly heights."

"Would you miss me?" he teased, squeezing her waist.

A sound escaped her. Part of it, he thought, was amusement. "Bah! I hardly know ye, so how could I possibly miss ye?" Iona exclaimed, whilst a blush of embarrassment that matched her hair rushed across her cheeks. She finally turned her face up to look at Aiden before she softly continued. "Ye dinnae have tae keep such close care of me, my laird. I have walked this path a hundred times or more without any mishap."

"You will have to indulge me and my whims, Lady Iona. I did vow to protect you and your son, did I not?" he asked, gazing down upon her.

"Aye. I suppose ye did," she said, before she yelled out to her son. "Gregor, watch where ye be walking or I'll take ye tae task if ye stumble and hurt yerself!"

"Stop coddling me, mama. I am a grown man," he yelled back.

"Ye are far from grown, Gregor Ferguson, and dinnae forget it," Iona replied. She sighed. "He is going tae be the death of me."

"He is but attempting to prove his worth. He will be fine, Iona," Aiden replied, whilst his attention returned to the lad. "He is his father's son."

"Aye, the spitting image of Ewan, for certain. Have ye learned anything yet as tae who might have killed him?"

Aiden gave a low growl of frustration. "As much as I would like to tell you otherwise, unfortunately, I have nothing to report. You yourself saw me standing over his body but the deed had already been committed by the time I arrived. I heard someone yelling that the laird had been killed but my men were nowhere near the body. I am thinking the worst but have no proof or even any leads to who might have killed him."

"We may never learn, then, who the culprit was," Iona said, a catch in her voice that told Aiden of her sorrow. He hated to add to her torment.

He halted their progress along the narrow path. "There is more…"

She wiped at her unfallen tears before she raised her head to stare upon him. "More?"

"Aye. I am afraid so," he murmured, unsure how to tell her of his latest news.

"Out with it then," she ordered.

"'Tis Broden… he escaped from his cell."

"Escaped?" she gasped.

"Aye, obviously with some help. But again, I have no clue as to who might have aided him," Aiden replied.

Iona cursed beneath her breath. "He will have gone into hiding in the village. There are enough of his supporters tae allow him tae disappear for weeks on end. If he does not wish tae be found, we willna find him."

"I can get my knights to go hut by hut—"

"—and make ye more of an enemy than ye already appear if ye raid their homes," she finished with a shake of her head. "Ye did want me being by yer side tae be a show of camaraderie, did ye not?"

They began to move forward again, and he was thankful when they reached the mainland. "Aye, of course, 'twas my plan. 'Tis my greatest hope that, by being seen with you, 'twill put the clan and villagers at ease."

"Then keep tae yer plan, although I still have my doubts such a ploy will work. Time is the only thing that may be in yer favor. Besides, that rat Broden will crawl out from whatever hole he is hiding in at some point. He craves attention and will surface when he can no longer stand when someone isnae fawning over him. He will also need time tae gather his forces tae try and take the castle from ye," Iona said before she raced ahead and took Gregor's hand.

Aiden shook his head at the sight of mother and son in the morning sunlight. He took a deep breath to calm his nerves for whatever awaited him in the village. A chuckle erupted behind him, and he turned to look over his shoulder. Finlay held back a further laugh and cleared his throat, attempting to look innocent.

Aiden frowned. "You have something to say?" he grumbled.

Finlay pointed to the boy. "The lad has more wits about him than most his age. Is he the same rascal who caught ye on the wall?"

"Aye," Aiden muttered, before swiping his hand over his neck, "and alerted the guards, the young pup! He has more gumption than most men I know."

"Ye shall have yer hands full with that one," Colin replied with his own amused tone.

Duncan's laughter joined the rest of the knights who stood watching the pair ahead of them. "Are we talking about the wee lad or the lady of the keep?"

Logan whistled. "She be a fine bonny lass that any man would be lucky tae call his wife!"

"Best not comment too much on the lady, my friends, or ye might feel the wrath of our new laird," Gavin chimed in. "He has it bad for her, if his frown is any indication of his feelings for the fair Iona."

Aiden had not realized he was frowning until Gavin mentioned it. "Enough! Keep an eye out for any mischief and above all that misbegotten cur, Broden."

"We are well aware how tae guard yer back, Aiden. We have been doing it for years," Finlay replied with another chuckle. "As if we could ever forget our duties…"

"Just be diligent," Aiden ordered. "I am still angry enough as it is. First that he escaped in the first place and second that my own damn guards were so lazy they allowed him to easily walk out my gates! Were they all sleeping or drinking the night away?"

Duncan growled his own frustration. "They have been reprimanded, Aiden. 'Twill not happen again."

"It best not or they will not see the light of day for weeks to come," Aiden warned with a heavy sigh. "Now let us catch up before we lose the lady and her son."

He hastened his pace until he strode up next to her as they continued their way to the village market. 'Twas a pleasant day, and when she took notice of a trinket or two, or a bunch of fabric, Aiden took out the necessary coins to pay for the items as soon as she moved on to the next stall. The blue colored fabric he sent back to the castle with Logan. 'Twould be a nice surprise when she returned to her chamber that day and the color would complement Iona's eyes once the material was made into a gown. Other trinkets included gifts for her son.

All in all, the day progressed much as Aiden had expected. Most of the villagers may have looked down their noses at him to begin with, but the coins Aiden was willing to put out for his purchases made a small difference. Most did not grumble too loudly about the source of their new found wealth. Iona's presence had also been most welcomed.

# CHAPTER 11

Iona's breath hitched in her throat when she opened her bedchamber door. There upon the bed were items she had fancied at the market this day. She forgot about Aiden, who stood at the door whilst she went to the side of her bed to stare down at the wealth of goods before her. Blue material she had admired that could be made into a gown. A necklace and a matching ring. Even ribbons of various colors for her hair. She raised her hand to her throat in indecision. Should she be upset that he had bought all this for her or happy that he cared enough to do so and part with his well-earned coins?

She turned to stare at the man, who still stood at the entrance to her chamber. A small smile lit his face and for a moment he appeared younger than usual. She guessed his age was similar to her own. He could not possibly be over a score and ten, or so she supposed. Yet. he always seemed older, as if the weight of the world was upon his shoulders . His brief smile stripped years off his age. She glanced back at the bed. He had parted with a fair amount of money for all these gifts… as long as he did not expect her favors in return.

"Ye parted with a large sum this day, my laird," she whispered, still trying to come to terms that this man before her was now the laird of Dunborough.

Aiden shrugged. "The cost is insignificant. Besides, the expense helped the clan and the local economy.

His words sounded cynical, but she could see he was attempting to hide his indifference to the cost he spent this day. "'Twas only to help the clan?" she probed, whilst waiting for his reply.

"Do the gifts make you happy?" he asked, stepping just inside the open portal.

"What woman would not like such gifts?" She came to stand before him.

"I care not for other women… only you. Do they make you happy, Iona?" Aiden took her hand and raised it to his lips until they touched her fingertips. His warm breath caused her to shiver in delight.

"Aye, as long as they are given freely and ye are not expecting anything from me in return," she replied honestly, although her heart raced with his nearness. When had been the last time a handsome man had caused such flutterings in her stomach? Long before Ewan, who had been much older than she. She thought it had been her first crush on a village lad when she was but a young girl. Had it truly been that long?

Aiden pulled her closer and she momentarily forget about denying anything he might offer her. Not when those mesmerizing violet eyes held hers in a hypnotizing grip. Her body flushed at being this close to him. He had unknowingly captured her affection, but she refused to let him know. His finger ran down her cheek and she did everything in her power not to give in to the spell he was casting around them.

"Are ye?" she murmured quietly, as she attempted to keep her wits about her.

"Am I what?" he asked, cupping her cheek.

She forced herself to step back and immediately felt the loss of the warmth of his body. "Are ye expecting anything from me for these gifts?" She waved her hand toward the bed.

Another smile crept across his features. "Nay. They are freely given to do with what you may, Iona. I would never ask anything from you that you were not ready to give."

"Then I thank ye for the gifts, my laird."

"Aiden…" he said, before turning toward the door. "I would ask that you call me by my given name as long as we are alone. Would you indulge me in this?"

She thought about his request. She supposed it was the least she could do. "Very well, Aiden. I thank ye for the gifts. 'Twas very thoughtful of ye."

"You are very welcome." He stood in the portal staring at her before continuing, "Will you do me the honor of joining me for the evening meal? I understand the cook has gone to extra lengths with whatever he has planned this eve. I assume 'tis for your benefit."

Iona nodded. "Since cook has gone tae such added efforts, how can I possibly deny such a request. I shall see ye shortly for the evening meal."

"I look forward to supping with you, my lady. Until then," he said with a nod.

Iona watched as Aiden disappeared down the passage before

she shut her bedchamber door and put the bolt into place. Leaning back against the solid wood, she raised her hand to her forehead wondering if she had a fever. Aiden had certainly lit a fire in her and Iona was not certain she wished for the flame to be extinguished. She must be mad, but then again, mayhap she should just enjoy being carefree for once in her life instead of being consumed by motherhood and the weight of all her responsibilities as wife to the laird.

The thought of Ewan, now dead in the cold earth, filled her with doubt. She reassured herself that he would certainly wish for her to go on with her life. That said, he may not have approved of Aiden as her choice. True, he was the invading enemy, and she should hate him, but somehow her heart softened whenever he was near. 'Twas as though the ice that encased her heart cracked each time she saw him. He was chipping away at the barrier and did not even know it. Or mayhap he did, given the attention he had given her this day.

When had she started to care for him? Mayhap 'twas the very night he took over the castle. She could forgive him for tying her up as long as she could forgive herself and the guilt she still felt for the betrayal of possibly falling for her enemy. *Enemy...* was he truly her enemy? Broden was for sure, the cowardly cur. That he was loose somewhere was Iona's biggest concern. Until the wretch was found, she would need to be on her guard. She had no doubt her brother-in-law was up to no good and he would only be too pleased to capture her or her son. Aye... Gregor could be used as leverage against her. They all needed to be cautious where Broden was concerned.

She pulled off her gown and used the water left in a basin to clean away the dust that had accumulated on her skin. Once she was clean, she toweled herself dry and went to the wooden chest at the foot of her bed. She pulled out a light green gown with embroidered flowers at the hem, sleeves, and neckline. 'Twas one of her best garments and she pondered whether Aiden would notice her efforts.

Her eyes went to the bed and the treasures that had been left there for her perusal. Green gemstones gleamed in the torchlight, and she smiled at how perfectly the jewelry matched what she planned to wear. A knock on her door caused her to pause. She called out, only to hear her maid on the other side. She slid the bolt and stood behind the door whilst allowing the girl to enter.

Before long, Iona was ready. Her hair had been pulled up with green ribbons whilst loose waves flowed down to her waist. She twirled around, marveling at how beautiful she felt. When had she ever felt this way? Ewan had never been one to give flowery comments, although he had been attentive to her needs. Tonight, she dressed for herself and whatever life had in store for her.

Leaving her bedchamber, she made her way down the passageway to the turret. The round stairs took her to the lower floors and soon she reached the bottom. Voices reached her ears, and she knew the great hall was filled with knights, ladies and some of the clan. She took a deep breath before making her entrance into the room. This was it... the moment that would change her life for either better or worse. She was about to show her choice for her future. All who saw her would know she had cast her fate with one who could still be considered their enemy.

Each step caused her heart to race, but she was determined

to put up a united front so that the new laird and the clan could find a common accord. She would be the bridge between them. Conversations began to dim when she made her way through the hall to stand before the raised dais.

One of the serving maids, Thora, was filling Aiden's chalice. Once she finished, she whispered in his ear. Iona couldn't hear what she said, but she could imagine it, considering the woman's bodice was all but open for all to see her overflowing breasts. Iona attempted not to scowl or allow the tiny bit of jealousy in her heart to show. Nay, she would not give the lass the satisfaction of exposing such a wicked emotion to cross her face. Instead, Iona smiled and dropped down into a deep curtsey.

"Lady Iona, you honor us with your presence this eve. I would be humbly grateful for you to sup with me and my personal guardsmen," Aiden said, loud enough for all to hear.

"My Laird Aiden," Iona replied as she stood. "I would be honored tae dine with ye and yer men."

Aiden had risen from his chair whilst he spoke. He now held out his hand for her. Iona made her way around the dais, up the steps, and took his hand, which he raised to his lips. "Pour Lady Iona wine," he ordered the woman who had thought to capture his attention.

"Aye, my laird," Thora said, filling another chalice. The woman frowned at Iona before heading back into the kitchen.

Iona took her seat next to Aiden and he moved a trencher between them to share. He waved his hand and soon the hall was filled with the aroma of all sorts of meats and other dishes to satisfy those who were there to break their fast.

Aiden reached out to place the choicest of meats on her side of the trencher. He then took his cup and raised it in a toast to the lady at his side. "To new beginnings."

Iona took her chalice and raised it to Aiden's. "Tae new beginnings," she repeated as they clinked their cups together. They each took a sip. He continued to stare upon Iona, and she blushed once more.

"Let us sup," Aiden said and took his fork and began to eat.

Iona nibbled at the food. She was so nervous. she was afraid to eat but the wine seemed to calm her nerves. And then Aiden spoke quietly so as not to be overheard by the other diners. His words sounded as if he had heard her innermost thoughts.

"If you do not eat and only drink this eve, you will regret it come the morn, my lady. Trust me when I say that drinking away your troubles will not solve anything. What is bothering you this night, Iona?"

She set her chalice down and took another bite of venison to appease him. She turned to look at the man she barely knew. "I fear I am not myself of late," she began, setting down her fork. "Ye have taken over my home and my emotions have been torn asunder. Does this make sense tae ye?" she asked with wide eyes.

Aiden turned in his chair to fully look upon her. He took her hands, and his thumb ran over the back. "Of course, I understand. I must needs admit I have felt an instant connection with you, Iona. Whether this is right or wrong in the eyes of our people, only time will tell. But know this… I have promised you and your son my protection. I will keep that vow to my last dying breath whether you and I form a relationship or not."

"Our people…" she murmured looking out into the hall. "Ye consider the clan and the villagers yer people?"

He nodded his head before answering her. "Of course, I do. They are mine to protect, along with these lands."

"In the name of an English king," she replied scowling. "I am not certain this will gain ye their favor, Aiden."

"I like the sound of my name as it passes your lips," he said, with a grin."

"And ye have not responded tae my most important statement."

"And you have not answered your thoughts about being in a relationship with me," he countered.

"I am not certain a response is needed."

"I suppose my reply about the lands I must now look over is of more import to you," he said, and at her nod, he continued. "I will be blunt, Iona. Although I was assigned this task, the part of me that is half Scot is warring with the other half of myself that is half English on my mother's side. King Henry may have asked me to take over this land in his name, but he is dealing with enough problems in his own family. His sons are not of a common accord. King Henry demanded his sons Richard and Geoffrey give homage for their lands to his heir, Henry the Younger, but Young Henry refused to accept."

"That could not have gone over well with yer king," she replied, taking another bite of the food set before her.

"Nay, it has not, at least according to what I have been privy to. I understand that war has broken out with King Henry and his son Richard. The King is about to embark to Aquitaine in a joint campaign. I was only too happy to not be asked to join them. I have no desire to be sent to France to take part in a war to satisfy others."

"And yet here ye are… conquering land belonging to another," she replied quietly.

"With as little bloodshed as humanly possible. I had no desire to take the lives of those who would eventually serve me. I suppose this is the way of life, but at least 'twas not a full siege that could have left those who reside within these walls and those in the village starving for months on end."

"Hopefully the clan will see yer logic, even though they failed tae defend the very walls that keep them safe."

"'Tis my greatest desire that we can all live in peace together, whether I serve an English king or a Scottish one," he said, also lifting his chalice to his lips.

"Ye think ye may come tae favor King William?" she asked, startled that he would even consider serving the Scottish king.

He gave a short laugh. "Miracles do happen, Iona," he said, setting his chalice down. "Hence my comment about both halves of me warring with each other. I am a Scotsman at heart, despite what you may think of me."

"Ye hardly sound like one."

"My accent does tend to come out when I am angry or upset, which hopefully you will not hear too often. But come… you have not answered me about a possible relationship between us. Do you think you might come to favor me in time?"

She considered his comment and could hardly deny the feelings between them. "'Tis a possibility, my laird," she replied honestly.

"Then all I ask is that you give us a chance," he said, taking her hand again and raising her fingertips to his lips.

Tingling sensations ran up her arm and she hated when he let go of her hand and returned to his meal. Her fingers shook when she picked up her fork to do the same. Aye... she may have said 'twas a possibility they could have a relationship between them but Iona already knew she was lost. Lost in a pair of violet eyes that would certainly be her undoing. She was in big trouble where the new laird of Dunborough was concerned.

# CHAPTER 12

*A*s they whirled around the floor, Aiden lifted Iona high then set her back down, following the patterns of the dance. Her laughter was infectious, and he was pleased he was the cause. Her blue eyes sparkled from the reflection of the torches hanging from the scones on the walls. Her loose red hair fell in soft waves down to her waist. As lady of the hall, she was gloriously in her element. She would keep that station in life if Aiden had anything to say about it.

The minstrels finished their song and Aiden was reluctant to let the lady go. Finlay came to bow before them. "May I have the next dance, my lady? That is, with Laird Aiden's permission," he asked politely.

"'Tis the lady's choice," Aiden replied with a bow.

"I would be delighted, Sir Finlay." Iona took his hand but peered over her shoulder to Aiden. She gave him a look that silently told him she, too, was sorry to leave his side.

He nodded again and reluctantly took his leave of the dance

floor. The minstrels took up their lutes and pipes and began to play again. Aiden returned to his place on the dais, holding out his cup to be refilled with wine. The same serving maid came up to him, but he barely paid her any attention whilst she filled his cup to the brim. Her hand made its way to caress his back. He raised one brow whilst peering over his shoulder.

"My name is Thora. Be there anything else, my laird, that I can get fer ye?" the girl asked all but spilling out of her tunic.

"Nay. I require nothing from you," he said sharply, hoping this would put an end to whatever she had in mind.

"Are ye sure? I am most willing tae see tae yer needs." She lingered close enough to him that Aiden became annoyed.

"As I said, I need nothing from you other than the wine."

She muffled her reply and took her leave. Aiden was grateful he did not need to deal further with the situation. He had no desire to dally with another. Not when he was devoted to the idea that he and Iona could come to terms. Aye... he had feelings for her, that much was certain. He had waited all his life for a woman to interest him and he would not be foolish enough to let a serving maid come between him and the woman he could come to love.

*Love...* He could not think of the last time he had considered such an emotion. 'Twas not that he had not succumbed to a woman or two to take care of his basic needs, but he had never allowed love to enter his heart. He never had the time. Not when he was doing everything in his power to make a name for himself or earn the favor of a king who may even now have forgotten about him.

King Henry was going to war, that much was certain. Would he truly remember his promise to give Aiden a title if he took over Dunborough? Most likely not, so what choice did Aiden have than to look to King William for his favor? He was not certain the Scottish king would think kindly of Aiden, considering he overtook this land.

He was undoubtedly in the middle of a conundrum. Aiden should be concentrating on earning the respect of the people he would now govern and not the swaying hips of a lovely woman. Yet how could he not think of the beauty who danced along to the tunes of a favorite Scottish song? Iona was perfection and yet she did not think of herself in such a way. That much Aiden was certainly aware of. He had seen for himself that she put the people and her son first. Could she possibly let Aiden into her heart? Only time would tell. He watched from his place at the dais whilst one clansman after another took Finlay's place.

Colin took the seat next to Aiden. "She is lovely," he said.

"Aye, she is," he replied as he watched the lady following the patterns of the dance with an unknown clansman.

"I am surprised ye allowed her tae dance with another. I thought ye would all but claim her for yerself this eve."

"If I am to win the people over, she must be allowed to make her own decisions. To be seen dancing with others besides myself is for the common good, even though I would prefer to keep her in my arms." Aiden ran his fingers over the back of his neck and then picked up his cup again. "There may not be enough wine in the cellars if I must needs only watch her the rest of the night."

Colin's mirth was evident given the loud chuckle that left his mouth. "'Twill indeed be a long night. Mayhap she will favor ye with another dance before 'tis over."

"Perchance... if I am that lucky," Aiden grumbled, before

Colin slapped him hard on the back. The force would have felled any other man.

"Mayhap she will favor me with the next dance."

"You will have to ask her yourself."

Without a by your leave, the music finished, and Colin left Aiden to go inquire if the lady would indeed favor him with a dance. He watched Iona laugh before she gave a curtsey and was again led to the floor. This time the tune was a slow one and Aiden grimaced as he watched his friend handle the lady.

Finlay returned to the table and took Colin's place. "Ye best ask her for the next dance or the whole damn clan will be in line for the lady's favor."

"She can make her own choices as to who she dances with," Aiden muttered in dismay.

"I seem tae remember another instance with a certain Captain of the Guard for the Devil's Dragon. Riorden de Deveraux was in the same predicament with his lady, if I recall. Do not be a fool and let yer lady slip through yer hands. Ask her for the next dance. I am certain she would rather be with ye than any other."

Aiden looked at his friend. "Do you really think so?"

"Aye, I do."

Aiden took another sip of his wine and then stood. Making his way to the minstrels, he leaned over to request another slow song when they finished. The man with the lute nodded and turned to the others as the music came to an end. Aiden crossed the floor and held out his hand to Iona.

"Would you do me the honor, Iona," he asked with a smile.

"Of course, my laird. I thought ye would never ask." She

placed her hand in his. His wave toward the minstrels had them taking up their instruments again.

He was happy to have the lady back in his arms. A slow tune allowed them the opportunity to have a conversation instead of passing snippets as they came together in the dance and parted again. "I am happy you accepted my request."

"Ye asked for another slow song, it appears. I am thankful for the change of pace."

"I could not have Colin be the only one to hold you close," he replied, pulling her a bit nearer. She did not complain or step away from him, which he took as a promising sign.

"I would have saved all of my dances just for ye if ye had but asked." Her hand reached up to touch the edges of his hair and she blushed and placed her hand back down upon his shoulder.

"Mayhap you would favor me with a walk outside for a bit." His offer was heartfelt, and he prayed she would feel comfortable enough to be alone with him.

Her smile crept across her face. "I would like that very much, Aiden."

Inwardly, he sighed in relief, and he continued to relish having Iona in his arms whilst they continued their dance together. 'Twas short lived, however, and when the music finished, he took her hand, placing it on his arm whilst he led her from the floor and back toward the dais. Her wine was still there, and she took a sip before looking upon him.

"I will need tae fetch my cloak since I am certain 'twill be chilly outside," she stated as she placed her cup back down.

"Then I will need to grab mine as well. Perchance a walk on the battlement walls is in order then, since we will already be climbing the turret stairs," he suggested.

"That sounds lovely. Shall we?" she asked.

He nodded and led her toward the turret stairs. At her bedchamber, he opened the door for her, and he waited whilst she went into the trunk at the foot of her bed and pulled out a woolen cloak. She quickly placed it around her shoulders but fumbled with the clasp.

"May I be of assistance?" he inquired with a grin, as he easily fastened the clap.

"Thank you, my laird."

Several doors down, they stopped at his own chamber door. "I will be but a moment." He, too, entered the room and went toward a chair where he had earlier left his cloak. Once donned, he left his bedchamber and took Iona's hand, leading her back to the turret. They climbed the remainder of the stairs and, as he opened the final door, a blast of cold ocean air met them. He saw Iona shiver and he placed his arm around her to keep her warm.

She turned her face upward and gave him an enchanting smile and his own face brightened that she did not protest being brought close to his side. They began to walk the battlements until they reached the part of the wall facing most of the moon lit ocean. He nodded his head toward the guards who were nearby. They took the hint and disappeared further along the walkway, leaving him and Iona in privacy.

He took Iona's hand and brought it to his lips. "I am glad you wished to join me here this eve, Iona," Aiden stated honestly and with an open heart. "You give me hope for a future together."

She turned her face upward again to stare at him with those wonderous blue eyes. A man could get lost in such a look. "I am still uncertain if this will work out between us, Aiden," she whispered.

"Do you fear me?" he asked hoping that this was not the cause of her apprehension.

"Nay, I do not, nor do I fear any man," she replied, jutting out her chin, "even when ye tied me tae that chair."

"'Twas a necessity, I assure you, and now highly regretted on my part. Can you forgive me?" Her bravery was to be applauded and was most likely the reason he was drawn to her. A woman who could stand up to him and share her thoughts was appealing to Aiden. He would never be able to stand a wife who cowered down to him for the rest of their lives.

"Mayhap... I suppose this is why I am here, is it not? Tae show a common accord for our people but also tae listen..." Her words faded away and she stared out into the distant horizon shining in the moonlight. Aiden could only wonder where her thoughts had wandered to.

"Listen to what, Iona?' he finally asked. He took his hand to her chin, so she had no option but to stare back at him.

She gave a heavy sigh. "Sometimes ye need tae listen when yer heart begins tae sing elsewise ye deny a part of yerself."

Aiden smiled as she confessed her inner most thoughts. "Your heart sings... a lovely analogy, Iona, as my heart is also singing just for you, if you care to listen hard enough."

"Ye are not jesting with me?"

He ran his finger down her cheek. "Nay! Never."

Her own smile crept across her face, and she placed her hand over his heart. "'Tis a bit of a predicament I am entering if I give my heart tae ye, my laird. If I trust ye with its keeping, will ye be crushing my spirits at some later point in time?"

"'Twould never be my intention to hurt you, Iona."

"Then perchance all will work out between us," she whispered, taking a step closer.

His arm wound itself around her waist bringing them just a breath away from being chest to chest. That she did not make any attempt to disentangle herself was another good sign, Aiden thought. He would take a leap of faith and, as he leaned forward, his lips were but inches from her own. He waited, holding his breath until Iona took that final step forward. She wound her arm around his neck and gently pushed the back of his head allowing their lips to meet in a gentle first kiss.

'Twas brief and Aiden rested his forehead upon Iona's whilst his heart raced at this first intimate meeting between them. He wanted more but did not wish to rush her. Afraid she might bolt if given the opportunity, or come to regret their kiss, Aiden again waited to see if she, too, wished for their kiss to continue.

Iona's breathing was as labored as his own and mayhap this was his answer. Her fingers playfully lingered in the edges of his hair until one hand came down over his shoulder to his chest to rest once more over his heart. Blue eyes met violet and, with a smile of encouragement from the lady, Aiden once more dipped his head down to kiss those waiting lips. There was nothing gentle about this encounter when Iona all but molded herself into his body. Aiden pulled the woman as close as he could whilst their kiss continued. His tongue swept over the crease of her lips and when she opened her mouth to him 'twas as though a winter rose blossomed in the spring air. A low moan escaped her, and Aiden knew she was as affected by their kiss as he was. 'Twas as though he all but claimed her... nay... they claimed each other, if he read all of Iona's reactions correctly. His heart soared at the thought she might one day be his completely.

With thoughts of Iona coming to care for him, his hands ran through the red tresses flowing down her back until he knew he was taking this a mite farther than he had originally intended. The reason? A part of him rose in anticipation of what could happen with but a simple word from the lady. He could possibly ask her to join him in his bedchamber. But he had the notion that this would only put a wedge between them and threaten what could possibly be perfect. He must needs be patient only long enough to allow Iona to come to terms with how their relationship might progress. He was not looking for some woman to warm his bed for a night or two. Nay! He wanted Iona and he wanted her as his wife for all time.

Such a revelation gave Aiden the strength to pull back and put an end to a kiss that begged to become more but could undo all his plans if he followed his baser urges. Her face reflected her disappointment, so there was some sense of satisfaction she felt the same way. He brushed her hair from her temple before placing a small kiss there.

"You must be cold, and the hour grows late," he said wishing he could keep her near.

"Aye. I should see tae Gregor and ensure he is abed." Her hand lifted to his cheek, and she kept it there whilst smiling into his eyes. "I have enjoyed the eve with ye, Aiden."

"As I have enjoyed our time together as well, Iona. Let me escort you down to your son's chamber and then to your own so you might take your ease."

Aiden took her hand, and they made their way to the turret stairs, but not before he made a motion to the nearby guards to begin their patrol once more. He was still wary of what Broden Ferguson was up to. Until the scoundrel was once more captured, Aiden would continue to be on guard.

Broden stood on the edge of the cliff watching the silhouette of the couple who had been locked in each other's arms. He spat on the ground before turning from the sight. He would recognize the shadow of Iona anywhere and he cursed that another had claimed her lips in a kiss that should have been his. But 'twas of no matter. Given enough time, Iona would be his as would these lands. He had not killed his own brother to lose all he coveted to an Englishman.

He raised his fist heaven bound and made a vow he would do all in his power to claim everything he had fought so hard for, or he would die trying.

# CHAPTER 13

Several days later, Aiden stood in his solar. The shutter to the window was flung wide open as if the breeze from the ocean would calm his anger. He had been roused from his bed before the sun had even come up and even now, only a bare glimpse of the shining orange globe touched the horizon. He took a deep breath and squared his shoulders before turning his attention back to the occupants of the room. He would show no weakness in front of the men whose loyalty he hoped to gain.

"He was caught attempting to sneak back into the castle this morn, my laird," Seamus said, frowning down at the man on the floor.

"And just who is this man you hold hostage before me?" Aiden asked, crossing his arms across his chest.

"Angus of Clan Ferguson, ye mindless cur," the man spat.

Seamus smacked the man on the back of the head. "Watch yer tongue!" he warned. A growl of outrage came from Angus.

"Ye bastard," Angus swore at Seamus. "Ye betray yer own kin by following this scum!"

Seamus ignored his outburst. "He is also friends with Broden. If anyone knows the whereabouts of Broden, 'twould be him."

Aiden raised his hand to his chin, contemplating Angus's fate. But mayhap 'twas not for him to decide but his own clan members. "I suspect he is not saying anything."

"Nay, my laird," Seamus replied, "although we have tried tae get the information from him. He's a stubborn lout."

A slight chuckle left Aiden. "I suspect I would be in the same position if our situations were reversed." Aiden's hands went behind his back. "Well, then… what do you propose we do with him, since he will not cooperate?"

Seamus's brow rose. "I am but the steward here. 'Tis not my place to pass judgement on him."

"I disagree," Aiden said carefully. "You are his kin. He will not reveal vital information we need to apprehend a man who escaped my dungeon most likely with the aid of this very man. Who else but one of his own should sentence him?"

Seamus opened and closed his mouth several times until he nodded. "Very well," he finally said. "Make an example of him then in the village square. Ten lashes."

"Ten? Is that not a bit extreme considering he very well may crack and reveal all with half that amount?" Aiden asked waiting for his steward's reply.

"Five then and not one less should serve as ample punishment. We would not wish to appear weak tae the clan," Seamus stated, hauling Angus to his feet.

Aiden nodded. "Take him away to the village. I will follow shortly to ensure the deed is carried out."

"Very well, my laird," Seamus replied. It took several men to remove Angus from the room. His curses were heard echoing in the passageway.

'Twas not the way to begin any morn and yet Aiden thought it had been fair to allow one of the clansmen to suggest the punishment. Now he would need to find another to carry out the deed. 'Twas no small task to whip a man. Five lashes might prove just enough to get the answers Aiden demanded.

He left the solar, stopping at his chamber to retrieve his cloak and sword. Strapping the belt about his waist, he inserted his blade into the scabbard and left his bedchamber to pass down the turret and through the great hall. He was met at the entrance to the keep by Logan and Colin along with several clansmen who nodded to him. One burly man had a whip attached to his own belt and Aiden knew he would not have to look for someone to inflict the punishment.

The way was still dark as they strode through the inner bailey and before they left through the barbican gate, he took up a torch. 'Twas an eerie sight as they made their way carefully across the pathway connecting the castle to the mainland. He briefly wondered how many years it might take before he would be comfortable treading this very path.

Once in the village square, Aiden saw that Angus was already tied to a tall wooden post. 'Twas clear to Aiden that this would not be the first prisoner who was made an example of. Angus's arms were stretched high above him, and he'd been stripped of his shirt. Aiden stepped forward.

"This man was caught attempting to sneak back into the castle. He has vital information regarding a prisoner who escaped the dungeon. He has refused to answer our questions as to Broden Ferguson's whereabouts." Aiden paced the crowd that began to gather. "One of your own has sentenced him to five lashes just as one of your own will perform the deed. If you are harboring Broden, you, too, will receive the taste of the lash. Proceed."

Aiden stepped back even whilst the crack of the whip hit the ground. Punishment would be swift, and he could only pray that mayhap once the first lash hit Angus's back, the man would reveal all.

# CHAPTER 14

*I*ona picked up her pace across the narrow spit of land. The sun had barely risen over the horizon, yet she was not one to dally in her room idling the day away. Besides, she had wanted to reach her cottage to pick up some of the things she had left there when she had thought she would no longer live at the castle. 'Twas not much but they were still her belongings and she wanted them with her, especially the few things she had kept as reminders of Ewan. They would someday be handed down to Gregor.

She reached the mainland, the dew still wet upon the ground, and turned to look behind her. Deidre, her lady in waiting, was lagging behind. She was carefully placing each step on the well-worn path. At this rate, they would not return to the keep until the noon meal.

"Hurry along with ye, Deidre. I dinnae have all day," she ordered, returning her attention to the village ahead of her. Several clansmen came running from their cottages, causing

Iona to wonder what was occurring in the village at such an hour. The men should be making their way to the fields. The village square would come alive with those attempting to sell their wares or with the children who would play whilst they could. Mayhap she should have awoken Gregor so that he, too, might find a bit of fun before the boys were forced to do their daily chores. She frowned. Something was going on and Iona did not have a good feeling.

Deidre caught up with her holding an empty basket. She was hoping to purchase vegetables for the evening meal for Cook. "Sorry for the delay, milady," she said, slightly out of breath and with a frown across her brow. "I hate that crossing."

"It takes some getting used tae even after all these years, but the narrowness of the path also keeps us safe," Iona replied, picking up her dress whilst just missing a pile of manure.

A snort left the lady next to her. "Bah! It hardly protected us from the damn English who have taken over. Why my sire, God rest his soul, would have had a fit tae know the place he called home was no longer in Scottish hands."

Iona came to an abrupt halt and turned to stare at her friend. "Ye cannae place blame on the new laird for obeying his king. 'Tis the way of the world. Lands change hands all the time," she chided shaking her finger at Deidre.

For the briefest instant a flash of fury crossed the older woman's face. "I can blame him! He is a traitor tae his Scottish ancestry, if what I have heard is true. If he had not come here, our men would not be buried in the cemetery and our true laird would as yet live. Ye remember him, Iona, do ye not?"

A gasp left Iona and she took a step back from the woman who had held her confidence for all the years she had been lady of the keep. "How dare ye say such a thing tae me! Do ye think I could forget my husband?"

Deidre started to walk, making Iona pick up her pace in order to continue their conversation. "I was just pondering the matter last eve, seeing as ye appear tae be very cozy with the new laird. Will there be a wedding soon? If so, some may also consider ye a traitor, too."

A sob escaped Iona as if her very own words had been voiced aloud. She could walk no further, and she watched Deidre continue onward without her. She supposed she could have given her lady in waiting a scathing retort and told her to mind her place. However, was not this the very reason Iona was awake at night? Torn between her love of the clan and her budding feelings for Aiden? Or was it the kiss she and Aiden had shared but three nights ago. Whatever the cause, the cruelty of Deidre's words made Iona wonder if she had lost the woman she considered her friend.

Iona had almost reached her cottage when the unmistakable sound of a whip, along with a man's cry, resounded in the air. She picked up her skirts to run in the direction of the town square only to see Tavish raising his arm to let the whip fly again. She ran forward and foolishly stood between the huge man and his target. The leather whip barely missed her.

"What is the meaning of this?" she cried out with hands on her hips.

"Iona!" Aiden called out quickly stepping forward and taking her by the arm. "Are you daft, woman, to put yourself in danger like this?"

She wretched her arm from Aiden's grasp. "Is this yer doing?" she bellowed pointing to Angus who moaned.

Aiden pulled her away to the edge of the crowd. "This is none of your concern," he hissed.

"Ye tie up one of my clansmen and then spout nonsense that this is not my business?" she fumed. "Ye are wrong, Aiden, if ye think I willnae voice my opinion on the matter!"

"Then mayhap you should give me the benefit of the doubt and ask me privately what is going on before you meddle in the middle of what your own clansman felt was a just punishment!" Aiden replied before raking his hand through his hair. "'Twas not my idea to have the man whipped, Iona."

"'Tis not right!" she said stomping her foot.

"Neither is helping Broden escape and keeping information on his whereabouts from me," Aiden retorted, before turning his attention back to the happenings in the square. "Proceed, Tavish."

Iona could not watch the rest of the proceedings and with a heavy heart, she continued to her cottage alone. The weight of her responsibilities to her son and clan consumed her entire being. She knew she could not help Angus but if what Aiden said was true, then the man held the answers as to where Broden was hiding. Once again, her heart was divided, and she could hardly begin to figure out where her loyalties should belong.

She opened the dwelling door and memories of when she had lived here with her parents filled her. She had been so young when they had perished of an illness Iona was lucky she did not catch herself. But she would not dwell on them now and instead begin to gather what she came for.

Inside the main bedroom, she went to a trunk sitting in the corner and lifted the lid. Her eyes misted when she espied

Ewan's shirts neatly folded, along with a signet ring that had belonged to his father. She held the silver in her palm. 'Twould be Gregor's now, once he was old enough to wear it. The satchel she had left here still remained on her bed and she picked it up and began placing various items inside she had planned to take with her. Ewan's things could remain here. She did not need his clothing as reminders of the time they had shared together.

She gazed toward the bed. Ewan's sword stood up against the wall. She went over to stare at the weapon for several minutes before she wrapped her fingers around the hilt. She barely managed to lift the heavy blade and she quickly put it back up against the wall. There was no way she would be able to carry Ewan's sword all the way back to the castle. 'Twould have to remain here until she could ask one of the clansmen to retrieve it for her. After all, 'twould also belong to Gregor one day.

Mayhap she should forget all that had transpired between her and the new laird and just remain here. She was so angry right now that such a thought held a fair amount of appeal. Yet, if she were to do so, then she would forget her original purpose and that was to unite the clan and Aiden's men so peace could reign. She shook her head, took one last look at her cottage, and then opened the door to leave. She had just shut the wooden portal behind her when she was grasped in a fierce grip, pulled around the corner of the cottage, and thrust up against the wall.

"Ye been cozying up tae our enemy, Iona, my sweet," Broden purred in her ear whilst his hand roamed over her body.

"Ye smell as though ye have been living with the pigs, Broden," she hissed, whilst attempting to put some distance from him. She was not wrong that the man's odor was horrendous and she almost gagged when his breath came near her mouth.

"Will ye not give me a taste of yer sweet lips, too?" His voice sounded strained, and Iona pushed at his chest, not that the man moved even an inch.

"Never!" she fumed angrily.

"I could take it from ye if I wished and no one would be the wiser," he threatened.

"And all I have tae do is scream," she warned and watched his eyes widened.

"Ye have not seen the last of me," he snapped before letting her go and quickly disappearing.

"Mores the pity," she murmured whilst picking up the satchel she had dropped.

She shivered thinking of Broden's body pressed up against her own. Obviously, he was hiding nearby. As angry as she was with Aiden, she pondered if she should tell him what had just happened and if she did not, would she come to regret it.

# CHAPTER 15

*A*iden was just finishing up brushing his horse when the familiar sound of a crunching apple filled the stable. He turned around to try and find the lad who surely must have a fondness for this particular fruit. The child's laughter filled the room and Aiden finally saw the boy in the loft above him, his feet swinging back and forth whilst he sat on the edge.

"Do you have nothing better to do than spy on me, Gregor?" Aiden asked closing the stall door.

The boy made his way down the ladder to stand at the closed stall. Aiden's horse lifted his head over the door and Gregor held out the remainder of his apple to the animal. Gregor then wiped his hand on his tunic and then stood staring at Aiden. "Thought ye mayhap might need help in here," he said.

"Perchance you should ask your mother. Certainly, she must need your aid with something," Aiden replied whilst he began to leave the stable.

"Nay. I heard she has locked herself in her bedchamber and is in a foul mood. Do ye have something tae do with that?" Gregor asked with hands on hips as he waited for Aiden to give his answer.

Aiden opened the massive door and then turned to peer down at the boy. "You have a fair amount of courage in you for one so young," Aiden murmured. He began making his way through the bailey.

Gregor followed closely behind. "Ye never answered me. Did ye make my mother mad? 'Tis never a good thing tae get on her bad side."

Aiden stopped his way up the keep steps. "If you must know, your mother is upset with me."

"Ye should make amends," Gregor urged.

"Mayhap she is the one who needs to make amends," Aiden said with a raised brow.

"Doesna matter," the boy stated as they made their way inside. "'Tis best ye make yer apologies. The longer she stews, the worst 'twill get."

"Is that so?" Aiden replied trying to keep the humor from his voice.

"Aye. 'Twill not go well for ye if ye wronged her. She be fierce when she is upset. But 'tis up tae ye what ye do."

Aiden nodded. "I will take what you said under advisement, young Gregor. Now off you go. I am certain you have better things to do than follow me around."

"Not really. Since ye have taken over, mother has forgotten about my lessons and such."

"What about being sent to another family so you can learn the duties of being a paige or squire?"

"My father never wanted me tae go tae my relatives. He never said why, not that it matters anymore." Gregor turned away from Aiden to hide his grief of losing his father.

Aiden took hold of the boy and gave him a hug. "I promise you, as I promised your mother, that I will find the culprit who killed your sire. This is my vow to you."

Gregor pulled away and his tear-streaked cheeks pulled at Aiden's heartstrings. "I believe ye, my laird. I hope ye find him soon and he rots in our dungeon."

The lad took off as if he had said all he had wanted to say, and Aiden could only ponder how he would fulfill this vow now also made to the young boy. He had no clue as to who might have killed the previous laird, but it would be in Aiden's best interest to find the murderer lest the same became his own fate.

Determined to right whatever wrong Iona was feeling towards him, Aiden made his way to her bedchamber. He was about to knock upon the wooden portal when Diedre, Iona's lady in waiting, opened the door to leave.

"Is Lady Iona available to talk?" Aiden asked and watched the woman tremble as though afraid of him.

"She is not inside," Diedre said curtly.

Aiden's brow lifted. "I mean your mistress no harm, but I was told she had taken to her chamber. If she is not inside, then where is she?"

Diedre's gaze swept up and down the passageway as if to find a way to escape. When no aid appeared, she frowned in resignation. "A servant informed me the lady had taken a satchel with herbs down tae the dungeon tae see tae Angus's wounds. If I had been here, I would have told her tae fetch the village healer but she's a stubborn one, our Iona is."

Aiden bit back a nasty retort. It would do no good to show any sign of weakness or anger toward this woman. He could see she struggled with divulging anything about Iona's whereabouts.

"I will fetch the lady myself to ensure no harm befalls her," Aiden said as he turned to head back to the stairs.

"And who will save her from yer advances, *my* laird?" the woman hissed before picking up the hem of her gown and making a hasty retreat down the dimly lit corridor.

There would be no friendship, if Aiden were to guess, coming from the woman. He shook off the hostility that still lingered in the air and began making his way downstairs. The great hall was mostly empty save a servant tending the fire and he wasted little time crossing the room and entering the kitchen. Cook was busy ordering the servants around as he worked on the evening meal, and Aiden again paid no mind to the chaos. He was too concerned with a red-haired beauty freezing herself to death in the cold lower areas of a musty dungeon.

He was about to descend into the bowels of the castle when he stopped a nearby servant coming out of the pantry. "Do we have a healer?" Aiden asked.

"Aye, my laird," the girl stated. "She has a hut on the outskirts of the village. Her name is Joan."

"Send someone quick to fetch her so she might tend a prisoner," Aiden ordered and then watched the girl scurry away to do his bidding.

He took a torch from the wall to light his way and began

making his way down the narrow set of steps. The lower he went, the cooler the air became until he, too, wondered at the wisdom of choosing to find the lady of the keep. Whispered words could finally be heard when he reached the bottom level and Aiden stayed in the shadows to observe Iona busily tending the moaning, injured man.

"Ye were a fool tae trust him, Angus," she scolded while dipping a cloth in a basin of water. "Whatever were ye thinking?"

"I wasna, milady. That be the problem." He hissed when she laid the linen on his torn flesh.

"Broden is worse than the scum beneath our feet. Ye would be smart tae stay well away from him," Iona counseled.

"He's been a friend…" Angus began then hissed when Iona laid another strip of linen on his back.

A snort left the lady's lips. "*Friend…* Broden Ferguson has no notion of the meaning of the word friend. He's a selfish lout who thinks only of himself and his own ambitions," she growled out, whilst wringing out another strip of linen from the basin of water and laying it on his back. "Do ye know where he is hiding?"

"Nay, milady," Angus replied.

"Ye would not lie tae me?" she asked, waiting for his reply.

"Nay, milady," Angus answered before adding, "He was hiding out in the barn at the far edge of the village, but I heard he's disappeared again."

Iona gave a heavy sigh. "I suppose the rat will surface again when it suits his mood and not before. Ye will tell us if ye hear anything."

"I am not likely tae learn of anything down here, milady," he said.

"I am certain Laird Aiden willna keep ye here for long. Not when ye can be of more use tae us above ground."

"Ye have my word I will help ye find him if given the chance. I have no notion tae taste the lash of the whip again for him or any who support him."

"Ye have made the right choice, Angus," she replied putting another strip across his back. "I am certain, since observing your punishment, not many would offer tae hide Broden. He is most likely on his own scavenging for food and finding a place to lay low."

"Not if they dinnae wish tae feel the lash…"

Aiden had heard enough, and he stepped forward into the light of the area. Several cells lined the stone walls but only one was currently occupied. "Come, Iona," he urged, holding out his hand to her. "I have asked someone to fetch the healer who should be down shortly to take care of Angus."

Her head rose from her task and her blue eyes reflected her gratitude. Cold fingers folded themselves into the palm of his hand whilst he helped her to her feet.

"He has no knowledge of where Broden is hiding, my laird," she said softly.

Aiden's brow lifted. "And do you believe him?"

"Aye. There is no reason for Angus tae tell us a falsehood. He has already felt the lash once. He has no desire tae feel such pain again," Iona answered, and Aiden saw her shiver. He put his arm around her, offering whatever warmth from his body he could share with the lady.

"Let us away and get you near a fire to warm yourself,"

Aiden murmured whilst turning to leave the dismal coldness of these lower levels of the keep.

"What of Angus?" she asked, turning to gaze upon the now still man who appeared as if he had passed out.

"I will have him moved to a chamber above to recuperate."

Iona nodded and Aiden escorted her toward the stairs just as Joan, the healer, was coming down them. "See to Angus's wounds and inform me once he is awake."

"Aye, my laird," she said firmly, whilst brushing past them and going to her patient.

They climbed the many stairs until they were once more on the level of the kitchen. The heavenly aroma of freshly baked bread and venison turning on a spit filled the room, causing Aiden's stomach to rumble. He led Iona into the great hall and settled her in a chair near the oversized hearth. He supposed the chair had previously been reserved for the lady of the keep. It seemed only fitting that she continued to use the chair at her leisure.

He saw she was comfortably settled with a blanket on her lap to take the chill from her body. He called for mulled wine and sent a servant to her bedchamber to retrieve a shawl for her shoulders. Once she was as comfortable as he could possibly make her, he took his own seat next to her and indulged in the idea of Iona one day being his in every way possible. He had never been one to think of his future with a wife by his side, but Iona made it easy for him to do so. Could his life really be so complete?

# CHAPTER 16

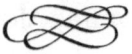

*B*roden waited impatiently in the shadows of the night. Those who had supported him in the past had dwindled to but a handful and he began to worry whether he could gather enough forces to take back the castle. Since his enemy had accomplished the deed with such a small force of men, Broden felt as though he was just as capable.

He knew every inch of Dunborough Castle more so than the current laird. But now that Angus had been captured, Broden began to fret, and rightly so. Angus had been the one person Broden had been able to count on to perform any task without question. Who knew how much information Angus had given away after the lash had met his back? Broden was unsure if he could still count on the man even if he were able to get him a missive.

He was tired of it all. After killing Ewan, he should have been living in the lap of luxury and sitting high and mighty as the new laird with Iona at his side. But nay! Even that right had been taken from him and he cursed Aiden of Berwyck and all those who sided with his enemy.

Even his own people had turned on him. The clan had seemingly fallen under the new laird's spell, making it harder for Broden to find someone willing to hide him in their dwellings. If this continued, Broden would have little choice but to leave these lands. All his efforts... all his scheming for years would have been for naught. He had to find a way to take back the keep and return to the clan's favor. The alternative was not an option in his mind.

A movement on the trail leading from the castle caught Broden's attention and he stepped forward from behind the village hut where he had been hiding. The figure came closer and Broden grinned. He at least had one person he could still depend on even if 'twas a woman.

"Yer late," he hissed, taking her arm and leading her into a nearby stable where they could talk in private. She yanked her arm from his grasp.

"And ye promised me I would be yer lady of the keep but here I am still a servant," she complained, whilst taking the hood from her head and pulling out her hair from beneath her cape.

Dark brown hair fell down past her shoulders and he was certain her brown eyes would mirror her mood. Clearly, she was just as upset as he was that his plans to take over the estate had not gone according to his plans. *Plans...* if he were honest with himself, he had no plans. Killing his brother had been but an opportunity seized when the enemy who had taken the castle were there to take the blame. As cozy as Iona had been, from his view of the couple on the battlement walls, it would not be long before the woman was bedded. By *Saint Michael's Wings*! What would it feel like to have her beneath him?

Thora stomped her foot whilst he had been lost in thought of Iona. "Well? When will ye make good on yer word tae have me as the lady in yer hall?"

He would need to placate this woman if he were to keep her happy so she would do his bidding. 'Twas clear the woman had not thought long enough about the fact that Broden owned no hall of his own... at least not as yet. "Now, now, my pet. Do not be so hasty. I promised ye would be my lady and so ye shall. We just need a wee bit of time so all my plans can come tae fruition," he coaxed whilst moving forward to take her in his arms. Leaning down, he kissed her lips all the while thinking of another he'd rather take to his bed. Such an act should have silenced her protests, but she was in a mood to be heard and Broden tempered down his rising annoyance at the girl.

"But ye promised, Broden," she whined softly, but the look in her eyes told him she was ready to give all to him with but a word or two of encouragement.

He reached inside his cloak and pulled out a small glass vial. "Ye must do me a favor, Thora, and begin placing a drop or two of this in the laird's wine. Not too much at once or those around MacLaren may become suspicious," he urged. He folded the poison into the palm of her hand.

She opened her fingers to stare upon the vial as if she had tasted of the concoction inside. She scowled at him. "But poison is a woman's method tae kill someone," she said fiercely. "Anyone with a bit of common sense will look tae those of us who serve him his meals!"

"There are many in the kitchens who could be responsible.

'Twill not necessarily point tae ye, my pet," he said, taking her fingers and once again closing the vial into her hand. "Do this favor for me, and all our dreams will be one step closer tae becoming a reality. Ye do wish tae please me, do ye not?"

"Of course, I do!" She gasped at his words before wrapping her arms around his waist and holding him close. His grin became wide, knowing he had won past any reservations she might have had.

"Ye are such a sweet thing," he whispered into her ear before walking backwards with her into a stall. He pushed her gently down into the straw before joining her. "Soon, ye will get everything ye deserve, my pet."

"Oh Broden! Ye make me so verra happy," she murmured. She reached up to place her hand on the back of his neck. "Kiss me, my laird, and take me now!"

A chuckle left his lips hearing the title that should have been his and he gave in to her demands. Aye… Thora would do his bidding and soon he would be well rid of her. *'Twill be so easy for an accident to befall the girl after she accomplishes all I require.* Accidents happened all the time, he mused. And once Thora had poisoned that bastard MacLaren, Broden would be there to easily replace him and then take Iona as his wife. He would then have everything he rightly deserved after having to live his life as a second son.

# CHAPTER 17

*I*ona watched the dancing in the great hall. A small smile swept across her lips whilst she observed Aiden dancing with one of the local ladies. He was an accomplished dancer, and she could find no fault with his steps in the Scottish dance.

Occasionally, there were moments throughout her day where she had the notion she should not be *this* happy. She should hate the man and the knights who had accompanied him to overtake their lands. Yet, Aiden made it so easy to forget he should be considered the clan's enemy instead of thinking how well he had adjusted to living here amongst them. Aye… even the Ferguson clan had taken a liking to the new laird of Dunborough Castle. Perchance, rightly so, since Aiden treated everyone fairly but still meted out punishment according to the crimes committed. He was more than capable of being laird of the castle and he proved each and every day that he would be a fair laird. They could not ask more from him than that.

Aiden smiled in her direction and gave her a jaunty salute as he continued the patterns of the dance. *The rogue!* Eyeing one lady whilst dancing with another should have repercussions, should they not? Yet, Iona could not stay mad at him for long. In fact, her heart betrayed her with the overwhelming emotions that welled up inside her every time she was in his presence. She was falling in love with him and could only pray that he would not end up breaking her heart.

The music ended, bringing Iona back to the present. She knew she would admit her feelings for Aiden only to herself. There was no sense in revealing anything to the man. Not at this point in whatever their relationship had become. True, the kiss they had shared had been most pleasant and, if she were to guess, Aiden would be just as talented in bed. Her face flushed with the thoughts of them lying naked upstairs in one of their bedchambers. Her fanciful thoughts had certainly taken hold of her, and she would need to forget them if she were to have any sort of a civil conversation with the man.

He began to approach the raised dais and Iona looked over her shoulder to one of the serving girls. "Thora," she called out trying not to think of the evening this same servant all but spilled out of her gown for Aiden's viewing. "Bring wine for our laird."

Thora nodded, raising the pitcher. "This one's empty, milady. I shall fetch another in the kitchen."

Iona waved the young woman off and welcomed Aiden to sit next to her. "Ye enjoyed the dancing, my laird?" she asked in a breathy whisper, as if she had been the one to be twirling around the floor with this handsome knight.

Aiden reached over to take her hand. His violet eyes never

left hers. "If only you had been the fair maiden on my arm," he murmured, appearing sincere with his words. "I would dance the entire night away with you, Iona, if I could."

She gave a merry laugh at the thought. "And deprive all these ladies just waiting for their turn with ye? I could never be so selfish as tae keep ye tae myself." His features grew serious, and Iona gulped whilst his eyes took on the look of a lover. His features all but spoke of his desires that surely must be a mirror of her own.

Aiden reached up to cup her cheek and her own hand lifted to gently cover his own. "There is only one woman here who has captured my attention. She is my match in every way. If possible, I would spend all my days, and most assuredly my nights, with her until my last dying breath."

A heavy sigh escaped her, knowing in her own heart that his words were honestly spoken. "Ye do not think we are taking things between us a might fast?" she asked, as a smidgen of doubt crept into her normal rational thinking.

"I think that mayhap the heart knows when a person has met the other half of themselves that has been missing. All things then fall into place. What does it matter if we have only just met or that we have known one another for years?" he inquired, whilst his thumb skimmed over her cheek.

"Some may say we are not thinking clearly," she said, although her thoughts were as clear as the day had been fair.

"I care not what others may think of us. I only know that you have been a pleasant surprise, Iona. I cherish our time together and look forward to what the future may bring." Another roguish grin lifted the corners of his mouth. He raised her hand toward his lips, turned her palm over and placed a kiss on her wrist.

There was no time for a response as a pitcher was pushed between them. Thora began pouring the wine into Aiden's chalice and Iona glared at the woman whilst watching her hands shake. Red wine spilled onto the white cloth.

"My apologies, my laird... milady," Thora said in a tone that was as shaky as her hands. "I will get something tae clean up my mess."

She flew from the table to disappear into the kitchen and did not reemerge. Aiden lifted his cup to his lips but, before he could take a sip, Iona reached over, turned the chalice and placed her lips where his had been but moments before. Aiden's eyes widened and then desire rushed across his visage whilst Iona took a long sip of his wine.

"'Tis a lover's gesture, Iona, to place your lips where mine had just touched this humble chalice," he murmured huskily.

"Aye, my laird, I am well aware of the custom," she replied, in a breathy whisper of desire. There was no sense in denying what she wanted and whom. Aiden fulfilled all of Iona's deepest yearnings for a chivalrous knight to call her very own. She might as well give in to the temptation he presented to her on a daily basis.

"And you choose now, of all times, when I must needs be present to fulfil my obligation to the clan and any woman who wishes to dance across the floor with the new laird?" he inquired. He gave a heavy sigh when he noticed another woman making her way toward the table. Iona noticed the woman was one among many who scrambled over who would gain Aiden's notice first.

Iona laughed brightly. "It seemed the safest solution, my laird, as I did not wish to get trampled in the rush for yer attention," she replied, before leaning forward to whisper in his ear. "However, the night's festivities will soon be over and perchance we can continue this discussion in one of our bedchambers."

"You will give me much to think on the rest of the eve, Iona. I can only pray the festivities will not last long." His breath was warm against her ear, and she held her breath when he placed a quick kiss upon her cheek.

Aiden quickly stood and was claimed by another woman from the clan. The dancing continued onward whilst Iona watched from a distance over the man she had come to care for. She drank his wine since he obviously had no need of it, occupied as he was, for it seemed every woman in the village, both young and old, came to claim their laird for a turn around the dance floor.

Her stomach revolted suddenly, and Iona quickly placed her hand over her mouth when she became nauseous. Peering at the leftover food, she wondered what on the trencher still before her had soured her stomach. 'Twas certain Aiden seemed to be fit and was not experiencing the same discomfort as he continued to hop and skip to the patterns of the current tune.

If not the food, then what? The wine? She had finished most of it by herself. Could it be... Iona frowned in thought. She was reaching for the cup when she felt as though she was about to lose her supper. She bolted from the room, running out through the kitchen doors to the garden since it was the closest exit, and she would never make it up to her bedchamber in time. She barely made it outside… the poor garden!

After losing the entire contents of her stomach, she made her way to her bedchamber. Once there, she took ink to parchment and sent her apologies to Aiden. She had had such lovely thoughts of spending the night in his arms and now they were all ruined. Making love was certainly not going to be the evening's entertainment, not when she was feeling this ill. Instead, Iona took off her gown, put on clean linen, and crawled between the coverings of her bed. 'Twould be a long time that night before she at last found her slumber.

# CHAPTER 18

$\mathcal{A}$iden worried over Iona whilst she slowly made her way to the table. The hall was mostly empty either from those who remained abed after too much to drink last eve, or those who had already eaten their fill of the morning meal and went about their daily tasks. For Aiden, he had been concerned after receiving Iona's missive. She had been unwell… or so her note alluded. At the time, Aiden thought perchance she had changed her mind about how their eve might progress. But a look at her pale face whilst she drew closer left Aiden in no doubt that whatever ailed her still had a hold of its effects on her.

She all but slumped into her chair next to him and pushed away the trencher he had moved between them. "Nothing so heavy this morn, Aiden," she whispered, covering her mouth.

He called out for porridge and soon a hot bowl was placed before her. "Mayhap this will settle your stomach."

She managed to lift one brow and her look told him much.

"Was it the food last eve that caused you to become unwell? Or mayhap you changed your mind, and your missive was an excuse." Hurt flashed across her features and Aiden regretted his words especially since he had noticed she was physically unwell.

"My only remorse was that I became ill. 'Twas certainly not my intent tae ruin what looked tae be a perfect eve once we were alone."

"My apologies, Iona. I did not mean to discount your words as an untruth."

"Yer apology is accepted, my laird."

Aiden gave her hand a squeeze. "The question still comes to mind what caused your discomfort."

Iona shrugged. "It could be any number of things, but I have my suspicions. Since ye partook of the same fare and appear as healthy as ever, then I am under the impression 'twas nothing I ate," she murmured lifting the spoon to her nose to sniff the contents. She hesitated and then sampled a small bite. Since another followed in its place, Aiden assumed the food agreed with her.

He nodded in her direction before beginning to eat from the trencher before him. "Then mayhap 'twas but an inconvenience and nothing to fret over."

"'Twas more than an upset stomach, my laird." Setting her spoon down, she sat back in her chair. "Not that this is the time for such a conversation whilst we are breaking our fast, but I felt as though my innards revoted against themselves last eve. I spent most of the eve with my head in a chamber pot. 'Twas most unpleasant."

"We shall hope for the best that your ailment has passed you by. Mayhap you are in need of fresh air to further remedy your recovery," he stated, when Thora came and placed a cup within his reach. He took hold of the tankard of ale, waited for Thora to depart, and then continued his conversation with Iona. "I would ask if you desire wine or ale but I have the notion neither would appeal to you this morn."

Aiden swore she turned a slight shade of green. "Nay. I shall refrain from drinking spirits this day," she began, before placing her hand on his arm and pressing down before he could take a sip of his drink. She leaned close. "Ye may wish tae rethink partaking of any drink coming from the kitchen. I fear yer wine or ale may be poisoned."

"Poisoned?" he bellowed.

"Shhh! Lower yer voice, Aiden, or all in sundry will know we have another traitor in our midst. Then we shall never flush out the scoundrel."

His sniffed the contents of his tankard but all he could smell was the heavenly scent of the contents of his cup. "Do you suppose Cook is out to tamper with just *my* food or all of the clan's meals?"

"I have known our cook all my life and never once doubted his loyalty to the clan. Nay. He is not the culprit."

"I would suspect Broden, but he is still out of reach, and no one will claim they have seen him in the village," Aiden said, now leery of both his drink and his food. He pushed the meat he had been enjoying around on his trencher before shoving the plate away.

Iona patted his arm. "Broden is most likely doing exactly what Broden is good at… intimidating people in order tae get his way. I have no doubt he has threatened everyone they will be killed unless they conceal his miserable hide. He will not have gone far, Aiden. I guarantee it. Not when he thinks he is still capable of taking this castle.

Aiden agreed with her assessment. "If not Broden, then who?" he asked scanning the room.

"I never said Broden was not responsible. He can still do much tae ensure someone he trusts performs according tae his demands," she replied with a scowl.

Aiden frowned. "Then it could be anyone who wishes to kill me... and I had thought that last night's festivities were a new beginning for us all. 'Twas stupid of me to think I would be so readily accepted as their new laird."

Iona pushed her chair closer so she could rest her head upon his shoulder. "'Twas not stupid tae wish our people would accept ye, Aiden. The person responsible for possibly poisoning ye is somewhere in this castle and 'tis not Angus. He is incapable of doing much except sleeping tae heal his back."

"He seems the likely choice. Are you certain?" Aiden asked.

"I would bet my life on it," she vowed. "Nay, we must needs look closer tae those who have access tae ye more readily. Thora is a likely choice but that almost seems a wee bit too obvious."

Aiden frowned. "Why would you suspect her? I have barely had anything to do with the woman."

Iona's brow rose. "Which is exactly why she may have a grudge against ye. A woman scorned and all that. Surely ye must know she favors ye?"

His gaze traveled to the young woman across the hall pouring wine into a raised chalice for one of the clansmen. "I cannot fathom why. I have not given her any reason to think I would favor her attention. Not when you and I have come to a common accord." He raised Iona's hand to his lips but then a crash across the room drew their attention to the sound. The glare Thora sent his way spoke much.

"Ye see? She does not like that ye give me yer attention. Mayhap we should find her other work that is not in the kitchens. She canna be trusted." Iona squeezed his hand until she went back to eating her porridge.

Mayhap Iona was right. Thora did bear watching, but whether her anger was only directed at him was questionable. For Iona had apparently not witnessed what he had briefly seen. The glare Thora tossed in their direction was not for Aiden alone. Thora also had something against Iona.

# CHAPTER 19

*I*ona flicked the reins of her horse as the mare galloped through the waves of the beach. Clumps of sand flew behind her to mark her way along the ocean's edge. She looked over her shoulder, hoping she had put a fair amount of distance between herself and the cocky knight who taunted her with a challenge that he would win a kiss from her. The distance to the forest was in sight and, despite her efforts and those of her horse, they were no match for the warhorse that carried Aiden's body as if there was no weight at all upon its back.

Aiden's laughter rang out when he came abreast of Iona, and she frowned. 'Twas not even a fair match! He was clearly holding his beast back.

"Ye are cheating!" she fumed, trying to sound cross though she was certain her laughter etched itself upon her features. She tried to hold back her merriment but was hard pressed to keep a straight face.

"I would never dare do something so unethical, my lady," Aiden returned placing his hand on his chest to appear crestfallen.

"Ye *are* cheating, ye heartless cur," she teased. "Ye hold back yer horse, Aiden! How is this a fair race if ye do not allow yer steed tae live up tae its full potential?"

Aiden's chuckle was infectious. "I but give you a fair attempt, my lady. This horse has carried me for many a year and in many battles. If I let him have the lead, I would even now be sitting beneath a tree yonder waiting for you to finally catch up so you might bestow upon me my reward."

"Ye shall never win my kiss, my laird," she called out, flicking her reins again in the possibility her mare might outrun the other horse.

Her hopes dimmed when Aiden shot forward. Her heart leapt into her throat whilst she watched as man and beast became one. Aiden leaned low in the saddle and his horse took off as though no words were necessary between them. Aye, Aiden was the horse's master and apparently the steed knew his owner well.

They left Iona alone on the beach and she pulled on the reins of her mare and gave her own animal a respite from its frantic trek across the strand. 'Twas clear she had been outmatched from the beginning. She might as well make Aiden wait as she took her sweet time to reach their agreed finishing point, where she would then have to concede.

He had already dismounted from his horse by the time she arrived. Aiden looked up at her like a man starving and she was his tasty treat. She swung her leg over the pommel whilst Aiden lifted his hands to help her down. As her body slid down along his muscled chest, she held her breath until her feet finally touched solid ground.

"I believe you owe me a kiss, my beautiful Iona." His husky whisper was almost her undoing, and she had to fight the urge to jump up into his arms to feel his body pressed against her own. 'Twas as though he read her thoughts, for his arm snaked around her waist, pulling her close.

"Do I?" she asked, playing with the edges of his red hair.

"Aye," he managed to say, "but only if you are willing to offer this humble knight such a magnificent reward."

He knew all the right words to tug at her heartstrings. She gave him what she hoped was a seductive smile. No further words were necessary between them. She gently put pressure on the back of his neck, so he had little choice other than to bend forward. His lips were so close to her own and still he waited for she knew not what. And then it dawned on her. Her kiss must be freely given. Her tongue flicked out to wet her lower lip and she swore she heard the man before her give a soft groan.

"Aiden…" His name came out as if from the depths of her very soul to reach out to the other half of herself that had been missing. She had waited an entire lifetime to find the man of her dreams. Now he stood within her arms, and she never wished to let him go again.

"Tell me what you desire, sweet Iona," he said. It touched her soul that he was willing to let her take control of whatever may follow between them. Not only was she more than ready to take these next steps with him, but his endearments touched her heart in a way Ewan's never did.

"Ye wish tae know what I desire?" she asked, whilst her fingers began to caress the edge of his leather jerkin.

"Aye... desperately," he replied, gulping whilst watching her every move.

She gave him a smile that hopefully bespoke all the emotions that were currently rushing through her body. "Perchance, we can begin with a kiss..."

His eyes seemingly gleamed in excitement as she repeated the words that were once his own. 'Twas apparently the only prompting he needed, and still Iona was unprepared when his head swooped downed to claim her lips in a kiss that rattled her core. His hands moved, and suddenly she was plastered against the rock-hard muscled frame that had tempted her since she met him. He was everything she had ever wanted in the man who would hopefully someday profess his love for her. *Love...* aye... the emotion that had evaded her for her entire life had finally found its way into her heart, brought there by the man who took possession of her mouth... her mind... and hopefully her body.

They moved as one, never losing their lips connection and yet Iona felt as though she was soaring through the air. Aiden's kiss was akin to magic and left her spellbound to this knight who had claimed her heart. He deepened their kiss and a moan of desire left her. She would give all to this man if he would but voice aloud his feelings for her. Aye... she was falling in love with him. Nevertheless, a part of her was afraid he did not feel the same. Would she regret their coupling if he made no promise to spend the rest of their lives together? Mayhap. She did not wish him to think her a loose woman who gave herself freely to any man of her choosing. Her doubts multiplied and drowned what she knew within her heart.

Aiden must have felt the uncertainty wreaking havoc with her mind for he halted the exquisite exploration of her mouth to stare down upon her with a frown. "Is aught amiss, Iona?" he asked, holding her at arm's length.

She lowered her head but hiding from him was not an option. He took hold of her chin and lifted her face to meet those incredible violet eyes. "N-nay... n-nothing is the matter, Aiden," she stammered.

He continued to watch her carefully. "Those luscious lips of yours are telling me a falsehood."

"Ye canna be certain of such a fact," she insisted whilst attempting to pull out of his arms. But he held her tightly and, honestly, she in truth did not wish to leave the security he offered.

"Aye, I can. You do not think I know you well enough to be able to tell when something is amiss?" he asked, but continued before she could answer. "One moment I had a willing woman in my arms and the next I was certain your ardor quickly cooled. What have I done wrong?"

Her shoulders sagged in her indecision about being honest with him. Would he laugh at her? There was only one way to be certain and that was to confess all. She took a deep breath and stared straight into those eyes that would most likely be her undoing.

"I will speak my concerns if only tae clear any uncertainties between us," she started, stepping back from him so she could assess his features in case he attempted to lie to her. The corners of his mouth lifted in a slight smile of encouragement.

"By all means… pray tell what concerns do you have, dearest Iona?" he inquired.

"'Tis only that I do not know yer intentions where ye and I are concerned. Am I only one woman among many who shall stir yer passion or am I someone ye wish to take to wife?" She shuffled her feet in the dirt, holding her breath whilst waiting for his reply.

His brow rose before he once again stepped closer to her. He ran a finger down her cheek and placed a quick kiss upon her lips. "My sweet Iona," he murmured, bringing her into his embrace and whispering in her ear. "I thought I had been showing you how much you have meant to me."

His hand ran over her hair, and she held tightly onto his waist. Her head rested on his chest to hear the fierce beating of his heart. "Ye must think me foolish tae voice such thoughts aloud."

"You? Foolish? Never," he declared. "But I thought you and I had come to an understanding, especially since you had hinted of visiting my bedchamber but recently. You are not some one-night dalliance, my dear."

She lifted her head from the comfort of his chest. "I am not?" she asked, with wide eyes.

He kissed her forehead. "Nay, you are not. I wish to make you my wife, Iona, and mayhap now is as good a time as any to ask you to be mine."

She bit her lip whilst her mind wandered over his words. "What of Gregor?" she inquired, hoping her son would be included in their lives. She could not imagine her child being sent away to foster in some unknown place.

"He is your son as he will be mine. Of course, I would expect him to be a part of our lives. Never doubt it." He hugged her close, resting his chin on the top of her head.

"Then ye care for me… for us?"

A chuckle rumbled in his chest. "Aye, Iona, I care for you both. I cannot in truth say that I am in love yet but given time I am certain the emotion will bring us both joy as we share our lives together," he replied. That certainly sounded like an honest answer.

"'Tis all I would ask of ye, Aiden," she said.

His palm cupped her cheek. "Will you marry me, Iona, and take me for your husband?"

She pulled back to look into his eyes. There did not appear to be any falsehood hiding within his features. Iona smiled and pulled on his jerkin, so he took another step closer. "I, too, have come tae care for ye, Aiden. Aye, I will marry ye. Now, kiss me and let us continue where we left off but moments before."

His kiss was short, and he chuckled when he saw her visage, which undoubtedly showed her disappointment. "Since you doubted my intentions, my dear, I think we shall wait to consummate our relationship until we are wed."

"But we do not have tae wait," she protested, thinking how much she wanted to share every part of her body with the knight in front of her.

"Aye, we do. Never let it be said I took unfair advantage over a lady… especially one whom I plan to make my bride. Now, come… let us return to the castle. We can find your son and tell him our good news."

She had no choice but to return to her horse and once Aiden

saw that she was settled in the saddle, they began to make their way back up the strand. The day that had started out in uncertainty of where their relationship was going had turned into a proposal of marriage. Aiden had not as yet declared his love, although neither had Iona, but she was sure that, too, would come in time.

# CHAPTER 20

*A*iden closed the latch on the stable door, gave his horse a pat on his muzzle, and saw that Gregor was attempting to do the same in the next stall. The pony Aiden had picked out for the lad had a mind of its own, however, and apparently knew Gregor had an apple hidden in his clothes. The boy's laughter rang out and he pulled from his tunic the fruit the horse had been begging for. One would have thought the young steed was a dog.

Aiden chuckled and came to the boy, pushed the pony back into the stall and put the bolt into place. "You did well in your lessons today, Gregor," he said, putting his arm around the lad's shoulders. "You will be a fine knight one day."

The boy looked up at him with hopeful eyes. "Do ye think so, my laird?" Gregor asked.

"Aye. The finest knight and mayhap a champion for our king," Aiden replied with a smile of encouragement.

"Which one?"

Aiden's world tilted with such a question. That was the conundrum surrounding Aiden's life now. He was completely torn in his duty to King Henry and his Scottish roots from his father's side of the family. How would his parents feel about the situation he had placed himself in if they yet lived? Certainly, one of them would be disappointed, given one had been English and the other a Scot. As each day passed into the next, Aiden was beginning to think that serving an English king would grant him nothing and mayhap he would be better off if he switched sides to serve King William.

"My laird?"

Lost in thought, he continued to mull over his predicament. Either side would consider Aiden a traitor. If he chose to side with Scotland, he would be hard pressed to ever set foot on English soil again. His thoughts wandered to his ancestral home of Berwyck Castle where his sister and husband resided. Resting on the border of both countries, the castle had been fought over by both sides over the centuries.

Berwyck was now claimed by England after the siege of 1174. Amiria was lucky to have fallen in love with King Henry's champion knight and still made it her home. Aye, Aiden had been bitter at first after losing his birthright. 'Twas the reason he had spent many a year in his attempts to make a name for himself and find a place to call home. He had come to a common accord with Dristan, Amiria's husband. After all, his sister was happily married and now had children of her own to raise. But if Aiden were to start a life with Iona and build his family with her in service to the King of Scotland, how could he ever endanger them or his sister by visiting Berwyck again?

The thought of never seeing his sister, or Berwyck for that matter, caused his head to ache.

"My laird... which king?" Gregor asked, tugging on the sleeve of Aiden's tunic.

Turning his thoughts away from a problem that became more complicated by the minute, he looked down upon the young boy. Gregor was of an impressionable age and Aiden did not wish to thrust his own problems on the boy.

He ruffled Gregor's hair. "'Twould be your choice, Gregor, of which king you would serve."

"Ye would let me choose, my laird?"

Aiden nodded. "'Twould be your decision," he repeated. They left the stable and Aiden shielded his eyes from the brightness of the sun. Gregor skipped ahead but then turned back to stare upon him.

"Ye were wise tae choose my mother for yer wife, my laird. Ye best be good tae her or ye shall answer to me," he warned, and his serious expression had Aiden holding back his amusement.

"I would expect no less from the man of the family," Aiden replied with his own sober look. He had no intention of ever hurting Iona or the young lad who smiled at Aiden's words. "Perchance with time you will call me by my given name."

Gregor's widened his eyes and he moved to stand before Aiden whilst continuing his assessment. "Huh. I thought for certain ye would make me call ye *father* or *papa*," he said, quietly. Clearly the boy was stunned but also there was a hint of loss shimmering in his eyes.

Aiden knelt down to be on the boy's own level. He took hold of one of Gregor's hands. "I can never, nor would I ever, attempt to replace your sire, Gregor. But mayhap, in time, you will begin to think of me as another father who shall raise you after your mother and I wed."

Gregor began walking backwards, a smug smile lighting his features as if only he was privy to some private joke. "We shall see... Aiden."

The boy's laughter rang out in the courtyard whilst Aiden stood watching the boy leave. He supposed he should take Gregor's words as a step in the right direction, since the lad departed calling Aiden by his given name.

Glaring at the sun, Aiden guessed he had time to peruse the documents that Seumas had left in his solar before heading to the training field. He stretched his arms over his head, knowing he needed to strengthen his sword arm and see that his men were fully trained. The keep loomed ahead, and he momentarily pondered where Iona was and what she was doing. He smiled as he took the stairs in the turret two at a time until he reached the floor housing the Ferguson family. He frowned, seeing Thora coming out from Iona's bedchamber with a pitcher in her hand.

Iona's suspicions filled his mind. "What are you doing here, Thora?" he shouted, coming to stand before the startled girl.

Her hands shook and the pitcher began to tumble toward the floor. Aiden caught it and frowned as red wine sloshed from the rim onto his clothes.

"One of the girls fell ill, my laird, and I offered tae fill in for her tae help with the cleaning," she replied, backing up from him.

Aiden stepped forward. "And you felt Lady Iona would need

wine if she returned to her chamber whilst you helped with the cleaning?"

"I did, my laird," she whispered with frantic eyes.

"I do not wish to see you on this floor again, Thora. Do I make myself clear?" he warned. The young woman bobbed her head before running down the passageway as fast as her feet would carry her.

Aiden scowled and then sniffed the contents of the wine, certain that it had been tampered with. Opening Iona's door, he went to the table where a cup waited and proceeded to pour the contents into a chamber pot. He opened the window shutter and poured the wine from the pitcher onto the grass below.

Aiden went about the remainder of his day. In time, the grass below Iona's window shriveled and died, looking as if it had been burned. By then, he no longer needed the evidence to prove Thora was out to poison Iona.

# CHAPTER 21

*B*roden stared in disbelief at the woman before him. All his plans were unraveling at a pace he could barely keep up with. He ran his hands over his face, whilst a growl of outrage left his lips.

"I just thought—" Thora began.

He roughly grabbed hold of Thora's arms and gave her a fierce shake. "That was yer first mistake, ye witless wench. Thinking!" he hissed through clenched teeth. "Tell me again what ye have foolishly done."

"'Twas not my fault that bitch drank MacLaren's wine," she fumed, wrenching her arms from his hands. She rubbed her limbs, most likely to remove the imprint of his fingers. He knew bruises would show by the morrow.

"Watch what ye call the lady," he ordered.

"Why? What do ye care what I call her? She has taken every-thing from me," Thora whined.

A snort left Broden's lips. "Ye think too highly of yerself if ye think ye could ever be in a position tae be lady of yonder keep."

Thora's eyes widened. "But ye told me…" her words trailed off whilst a frown formed on her brow.

His laugher rang out in the evening air and a twisted smile crept across his mouth. "And ye were stupid enough to believe me," he stated whilst he began to pace. "However, one mistake I can forgive. I willna be so lenient with a second. Why isn't MacLaren dead after ye have had two se'nnights tae kill the bastard?"

"I believe they may have suspected me after Iona took sick. I was removed from the kitchens and sent tae clean. Clean! I have been reduced tae the lowest of servants," she complained bitterly. "Ye were supposed tae make me the lady of the hall! Now, I am cleaning chamber pots filled with *shite* or putting parchment in the garderobes so the high and mighty can wipe their arses! I am not meant tae be doing chores such as this."

He raised his eyes toward the heavens as though asking God to give him strength, not that he believed God would be on his side when he wanted to see to someone's demise. He ignored her gripes and held out his hand. "Give me the rest of the poison and I will see MacLaren dead myself."

She shuffled her feet in the dirt beneath her shoes. "I do not see how ye can do a better job of it than I myself have tried when ye canna even gain access tae the castle. Besides… 'Tis gone."

Broden grabbed hold of her once again. "Gone? What do ye mean 'tis gone. There was enough in the vial I gave ye tae poison an entire garrison. I told ye tae use only a drop or two!"

She lifted her chin. "And I put the rest in a pitcher of wine tae serve Iona so I could get rid of her."

"Yer instructions were not tae kill Iona but the man who claims to be laird!' he shouted.

Thora shrugged. "She was in my way tae getting what I wanted. 'Tis not my fault MacLaren showed up when he did and took the rest of the poison from me. Hopefully, she will drink what I left in her bedchamber and that will be the end of her!"

A roar of outrage burst from the depths of his soul, and he turned furious eyes on the person who was the cause. "Ye had best wish that the lady did not consume the wine, for she will one day by my wife."

"Ye canna wed her. Not when ye promised me that I would be yer bride," she bellowed.

"I would have never wed ye. Yer a stupid woman who is beneath my contempt and my patience with ye is at an end. Ye have thwarted my plans for the last time," he said, even as his hand reached for her throat and squeezed.

There was a small bit of satisfaction in watching the woman claw feebly at his hand. Broden kept up the pressure until her head rolled to the side and she stared at him with sightless eyes. He tossed her to the ground, knowing she had thwarted his plans to gain what he desired.

He walked away, not giving the dead girl a second thought. Perchance there was another way to make Iona come to him, and willingly. He laughed as another plan began to form in his mind. This one would be too simple and yet it just might work.

# CHAPTER 22

*I*ona giggled like a young maiden whilst the two women pulled a gown over her head. The light green linen hugged her waist as the rest of the material fell to the floor. One of the women knelt down and began tugging at the hem in order to determine its length. Another pulled ribbons from a box for possible trim, although Iona thought embroidery at the end of the sleeves and neckline would be lovely. She wanted this gown to be perfect, for the dress would be the one she was to be married in.

A knock on the door had one of the ladies going to the portal and sliding the bolt. When they learned Aiden was on the other side, another quickly covered the dress so he would not see the gown.

"Ye canna come in, Aiden. I am trying on my dress," she said, moving across the room but hiding behind the wooden door.

"I would not dream of spoiling the moment when I first

espy you in the chapel, my dear, but there is an emergency I would greatly appreciate your counsel on," Aiden said quietly.

"Give me a moment to change and I will be with you shortly," Iona murmured, before turning to the ladies and clapping her hands. "I think flowered embroidery will suit the gown nicely. Help me get this off and into another gown," Iona declared, and the women nodded their agreement before pulling the fabric from her body.

Once changed from her wedding finery, Iona met Aiden in the passageway. He offered her his arm and they hurried down the corridor, to the turret stairs, and out the keep. They continued onward to the rear postern gate where knights standing guard bowed before opening the portal.

"Will you tell me what has happened, or should I guess?" she finally asked, whilst crossing the narrow path to the mainland.

He halted their progress. "There has been another murder," he said, before urging her forward and into the village. They kept silent until they met up with Finlay who stood over a body that had been covered with a blanket. He nodded to the man who uncovered the girl beneath.

A gasp left Iona as she knelt by the servant. "Thora!" she turned her head briefly to collect herself before turning her attention to the now cold, dead woman. "What happened?"

Aiden knelt by her side and pointed to her neck. "Strangled. But if that wasn't enough, the killer broke her neck, which explains the odd angle her head is resting."

"But who could have done such a deed? For the most part this woman was a harmless servant," she said. Aiden stood and helped her to rise next to him. He placed an arm around her shoulder for support.

"Our guess is whoever hired her to kill us. 'Tis clear she did not perform up to the standards of whomever was behind this."

"Broden," she hissed.

Finlay nodded. "Aye, 'tis our assumption, as well, which is why Aiden has doubled the patrols tae find the scoundrel."

Iona's brow rose and she raised her head to the man at her side. "We will need more effort on our part than tae double the guards. It hath not done us any good in finding the brute since my husband was killed. We are no closer tae finding him now than we were before, and now we have another murder on our hands. What could possibly be next?"

Finlay frowned. "You think he is up to more?"

A snort left her. "Of course, there is more," she answered, pointing down to the dead girl. "This is just another act tae get our attention. He will not quit until he has gotten what he wants... being laird of the castle. 'Twas always a sore point that he was not born first and was second to Ewan. But what is unclear, is what that madman will do next?"

Finlay spoke up as Aiden paced back and forth lost in thought. "I think we need tae double the guards surrounding the both of ye, my laird. Iona may have drunk the wine that poisoned her, but it was meant for ye. And ye also caught Thora coming out of Lady Iona's chamber... somewhere she had no place being."

Another gasp left her. "Ye did not mention this tae me, Aiden."

He kissed her temple. "My apologies, my lady, but I thought I had thwarted any plans she may have had, especially since I dumped what she left in your chamber out of the window."

"'Twas still important. I should have been told," she scolded.

"Again, I apologize, Iona. I did not wish to worry you."

She was satisfied... for the moment. "Mayhap Thora was acting on her own ambitions."

Both Finlay and Aiden's brows crossed at her words, but Finlay spoke up first. "Ye think her attempts on yer life was her plan and not Broden's?"

She waited a few moments until she at last spoke her mind. "I have not mentioned this before, but when Ewan yet lived, I spent much of my time attempting tae stay out of Broden's path. He always put me in uncomfortable positions and tended tae place his hands where they did not belong on my body." She looked down at these final words knowing what was to come next.

"And you did not think such information was of import," Aiden said, almost replicating her own words but moments before.

She looked at him sheepishly. "My apologies, Aiden, but at first 'twas not something I was willing tae discuss with a stranger who had just invaded my home. Then... I just wished tae forget the whole matter."

Finlay nodded to a few men who stood nearby with a wagon. They came over and took Thora's body to ready her for burial. "I think this just increased the importance of finding Broden," he stated as the three of them began to make their way back to the castle. "'Tis obvious the man has other ulterior motives where the lady is concerned... most likely making her his wife once he has again taken over the estate and clan."

"He would not dare!" Iona objected, more frightened than she was before, thinking of being in the hands of that monster.

Aiden nodded. "I agree. Double the guards around the lady and her son. Where is he, by the way?"

"He was here in the village playing with his friends," she said, worry now reflected in her eyes.

Aiden's own eyes widened before turning his attention to Finlay. "Find him, and quickly. Bring him back under close guard to the castle. Neither one is to leave the grounds until Broden is found.

Finlay bowed. "Aye, my laird. 'Twill be done."

As Iona and Aiden continued onward to the castle she could not help asking. "Ye do not think Broden would do anything tae my son, do ye?"

Iona felt Aiden pull her closer. "It stands to reason Broden will go to any lengths to see his will has been done. Taking your son would fit into his plans, I would think."

A cry left her. "Maybe we should help with finding him."

"I will not put you in further danger, my love. Nay, leave the finding of Gregor to Finlay and my guards. They will locate him and bring him home," Aiden replied, and she could only nod even whilst her gaze went back to the village behind her.

She should have gone herself. She should have listened to that small voice inside her head. Instead, she left her confidence in the man she loved, knowing he would do all in his power to ensure her son's safety.

# CHAPTER 23

*B*roden held tight to the squirming brat in his arms. He had suffered much during his attempts to take the boy and he should have known getting Gregor to come along quietly was going to be an issue. Still... he had bided his time, hiding beneath the shadows of the nearby trees whilst the boy played with his friends. Luck had been on Broden's side when the ball they had been throwing went over Gregor's head and his nephew ran directly toward Broden's place of hiding.

'Twas easy enough to snatch the boy's arm, or so Broden had thought until a well-aimed kick almost landed in his privates. Broden's hand swiftly moved to clamp his fingers over the boy's mouth. He succeeded, but only to have the boy leave teeth marks on his skin. He should have brought rope but there would have been no time to tie his nephew up, especially once Broden heard Gregor's name being called and he began to run deeper into the forest.

His lungs burned in his efforts to put as much distance

between him and the village where he had been hiding of late. He trusted no one, especially any of the clansmen in the village. The turncoats! Thora was dead, so clearly she would be no help to him in his latest plans. That was all the thought he gave to the woman who died at his own hands. Angus, whom he thought he could trust, had taken the whip on his behalf but Broden had the uncanny notion that expecting any further help from that quarter would also be useless. So how was he to take back what was rightfully his when any who had been on his side now seemingly renounced him?

Aye! He was alone and all his great plans after he killed his brother to claim the clan and land had twisted awry the instant he had escaped the dungeon. His only thought now was that, if he could not have the land, then at the very least he should be compensated for all he had lost. Ransoming his nephew seemed the next best course of action.

He neared the hut where he had been hiding. Little more than a hovel, the forest had all but claimed the dwelling, as the exterior walls were covered in moss and appeared as though they were ready to collapse. But Broden had taken some time to reinforce the walls as best he could, knowing this was only temporary.

He shoved Gregor through the doorway, sliding a bolt into place. He hoped to convince the boy that there was no place to go. Broden rubbed his sore hand whilst his nephew glared at him with his brother's eyes.

"Ye filthy cur!" Gregor cried out. "Just ye wait until my mother learns of yer deceit."

"Yer mother is the least of my worries," Broden snarled, knowing the lady was now hopelessly out of his reach. The taking of her son had seen to that, let alone that he killed her husband.

The boy crossed his arms over his chest. "Laird Aiden will come for me."

A sly smirk crept across Broden's mouth. "I am counting on it."

Confusion crossed the boy's features before he once more spoke his thoughts. "How can ye do this tae me, Uncle? We are family."

A snort left Broden's lips. "*Family*... we may share the same blood, but we are no longer family. Do ye wish tae know why?"

"Aye." Gregor's reply was but a whisper.

Broden knelt down so he could see straight into the boy's face. "Because the minute I killed my brother, I became yer enemy."

A startled cry was ripped from the boy's mouth. "W-why? W-why would ye k-kill my father?"

Broden shrugged before standing, whilst the boy began to cry. He made his way around the small room to gather a rope and a strip of linen. "He had what I wanted, including yer mother. Seemed tae make sense at the time."

Gregor looked up at him once he stood before him again. "Why are ye confessing this tae me?" the lad asked.

Broden knelt and began to tie his nephew up. Once the boy was secure, he held the strip of linen up to his face. "Someone should at least know the depths I have gone through in order tae acquire all that I desire. Now shut up. I have had enough of yer talking."

Broden left the boy where he was, knowing he was now secure and was not going anywhere. Gregor's sobbing meant nothing to him. He cared little for anyone at this point in his life. The only thing that matter was his own survival.

He went to the small table where parchment and quill awaited him and began to pen his missive. He may not have the keep, Iona, or control over the lands, but the new laird and his lady would pay dearly for the return of her son.

# CHAPTER 24

*A*iden threw the missive he had read aloud onto his desk in disgust. Was he surprised at the content? Not really, but that Gregor's own uncle would stoop so low as to kidnap a child and hold him for ransom was beyond appalling. Aiden had already sent someone to ask Iona to join him. He was certain her reaction would be to rush out from the safety of the castle to rescue her son.

He looked around at those who had gathered in his solar. Five men who had been with him since he could walk and one who had followed him after a tourney.

Logan strode across the room to pick up the discarded parchment. A growl of outrage left him. "'Tis a trap."

Colin nodded. "Of course, 'tis a trap, ye dolt."

"Anyone with any sense can see for themselves that whoever goes tae meet Broden will have tae fight for his life," Gavin chimed in.

Aiden ran his hand through his hair. "'Tis of the greatest import that we plan a rescue with the utmost of care."

"Aye," Finlay agreed. "The boy canna be harmed."

"She willna like being kept out of this discussion," Duncan said, whilst his gaze went toward the closed portal.

Aiden crossed his arms over his chest. "She has been sent for."

"She will want tae go," Colin stated.

Aiden shook his head, knowing he would in no way allow his lady anywhere near Broden. The man was a murderer and now had taken his own nephew. 'Twas clear he had no loyalty to his family or anyone else for that matter. "Nay. I go alone." Conversations erupted in the room whilst all the men began to voice their disapproval. He held up his hand to silence his friends. "You know this is going to be the best course of action. We cannot all just go traipsing to the rendezvous point of Broden's choosing. He might kill the boy and I will not put Iona's son in more danger than he already is in."

Finlay stepped forward. "And I canna in good faith let ye go alone!"

"Aye!" the men all chorused.

Aiden returned to his desk and unrolled a map of the area. Placing weights on the ends to hold the parchment in place, he motioned his knights forward. He scanned the layout of the land before pointing to the area where he was to meet Broden. "Our enemy thinks he knows how this whole endeavor will play out. Mayhap we can change what happens. He thinks he has the upper hand by demanding we meet at dusk when the light of day is almost at an end. He thinks this will give him the advantage, since he knows the area better. Perchance if you all arrive early and hide out, then I can appear as though I have arrived alone."

Logan fingered the hilt of the dagger attached to the belt at his waist. "I would like nothing better for the bloody cur tae feel the point of my blade."

"Aye!" Colin agreed. "There is no honor in a person who would use a child as leverage tae getting what he wants."

Finlay bent forward and frowned. "Ye would have us conceal ourselves too far away. Much could happen before we could reach ye or the boy."

Aiden scowled. "Do you have a better idea?"

Finlay pointed to another area of the map. "Here. 'Tis the higher ground and would give us an advantage. Post some of us here and others closer tae the ground so that we can rescue Gregor when the opportunity presents itself."

Duncan pointed to some nearby trees. "And this grove will be far closer than the one ye proposed. A few of us could hide here."

Colin shook his head. "But we do not know which direction Ferguson will be entering the glade. He may end up seeing us and then all will be lost, including the boy."

A grunt left Logan. "I am certain we are more than capable of repositioning ourselves in the event we hear our enemy's approach. I cannot image he will be able tae quietly enter the area where he is tae meet Aiden whilst dragging a child with him."

Duncan nodded. "Gregor is smart. I would expect him tae put up a fight."

"Aye," Finlay agreed. "The boy will know enough of his situation tae make as much noise as he is able."

"Ye will still be walking into a trap and will have tae fight yer way out of the situation," Gavin grumbled.

Aiden nodded. "As long as that bastard lies dead at my feet afterward, I am prepared to do all in my power to save Iona's son."

The solar door burst open, causing the men to give a small bow to the lady who filled the portal. Aiden witnessed her panic-filled eyes and motioned for his friends to leave. She rushed across the room and straight into his arms.

"Ye have news of my son?" she asked. Her body trembled and Aiden held her closer.

"Aye, but you will not like what I have to tell you." His answer was softly spoken to try to instill a sense of calm in Iona when he was anything but composed. In fact, Aiden was ready to explode in fury, not only with Broden but with himself for not capturing the fugitive right away. He should have seen the deed done first hand and not have left it to others. Regret filled his heart, especially knowing Gregor had trusted him to see to his and his mother's safety. He had failed them both.

"Where is he? Where is my son?" she cried out, holding onto his tunic as though for dear life.

"Mayhap you should sit, Iona," he suggested, pointing to a chair near the hearth.

"I do not want tae sit, Aiden. I want my son!"

He took her elbow and ushered her across the room where she at last took a seat. He went to pour her a cup of wine and held the offering out to her. Reluctantly, she took the chalice and a drink before handing it back to him. Folding her hand in her lap she waited for him to continue.

He returned to his desk to retrieve the missive and handed

her the parchment. A gasp filled the room once she had finished reading Broden's demands.

"The bastard!" she bellowed, whilst tears rushed unchecked down her cheeks. "I swear I could gut that fiend and not lose a moment's slumber."

Aiden sat next to her. "My thoughts exactly, my dear."

"I should change into something more suitable for travel," she said, wiping the wetness from her face.

"You, my sweet, are going nowhere near Broden," Aiden warned.

"But—"

"There is no *but* in this situation, Iona. On this matter I must stand firm," Aiden scowled, before standing to pace back and forth. "I will not lose you both. I have failed you now twice and must rectify the matter posthaste."

A frown marred her otherwise flawless brow. "Failed me? How?" she asked innocently.

He turned to gaze down upon her and then knelt before his lady, taking her hands in his. "Forgive me for not doing all in my power to find your brother-in-law when he first escaped. The responsibility was mine and I left the task to others."

"Of course, I forgive ye, Aiden. 'Tis not yer fault Gregor has been taken."

"Aye! 'Twas all my fault. If I had spent more time finding that cur instead of trying to mend my reputation with the clan and you, your son would even now be safe within the walls of our keep!"

"Ye regret how our relationship has progressed thus far?" she questioned with another frown.

"Nay. That is not what I meant. If I had done all in my

power to find Broden in the first place mayhap Gregor would now be safe."

Iona squeezed his hands as if she understood how he felt and wanted to comfort him. Her words proved that assessment. "Ye could not have known Broden would stoop so low as tae take my child in order tae gain the wealth in our coffers."

"Scum like Broden who would kill his own brother would do anything to gain his desires. He has no honor within him. Your son most likely provided as good as an excuse as any to ensure Broden's demands are met for the monies he thinks will gain him his riches."

"Ye think he killed Ewan?" she asked, with wide eyes.

"Think about it, Iona. You have told me there was no love lost between the brothers. It stands to reason that Broden would take advantage of the situation when I invaded the keep in the middle of the night. Chaos had erupted. My men and the castle knights were everywhere trying to take control. It would have been easy enough for Broden to kill your husband when his back was turned, and Ewan's attention was focused on saving his home and family."

"I canna fathom even Broden going so far..." her words trailed off as if she was lost deep in thought. "I must confess that I knew he wanted me for his own and would go tae any length tae have me. But only a fool would think I would immediately become the wife of my husband's brother after his death."

"I am not entirely certain Broden is of a right mind, my love, to think of anything other than what he wants," Aiden replied, then returned to his chair. "His missive at least did not demand your attendance and I will be grateful for that."

"I loathed the man before Ewan's death. Tae think he killed Ewan makes me wish tae see his demise at the end of yer sword."

"I want you nowhere near the battle between Broden and myself, Iona. Suffice to say, I will see his head on a pike outside our gates if this is your wish."

Iona shuddered. "Nothing so drastic, Aiden. I only wish tae know that the man who killed my husband and stole my son does not live tae see another day."

Aiden returned to her side and pulled her from her chair to envelope her in his arms. "I make my vow to you that I shall return your son safely to your side."

"And see that Broden is dead," she continued.

"Aye. Once I am done with him, hell will gladly take his soul to rot in its fiery pit."

She raised her head, and he bent down to touch his forehead to hers. "I vow this to you, Iona, and seal my promise with a kiss," Aiden whispered, moving his mouth to hover over her lips.

Without hesitation, she kissed him with all the passion that had blossomed between them since he first came to this land. Aye... he had made a solemn vow to her this day, and he would move heaven and earth to see that his words to her came true.

# CHAPTER 25

*B*roden came up to his nephew with a strip of linen in his hands. The boy clearly knew what was about to happen since he firmly pressed his lips together and threw Broden a defiant look of sheer hatred. But he would not allow a mere child to get his way. Nay! The boy would be gagged and Broden would see the matter done.

Inwardly, he was very pleased with himself. The appointed hour had come at last, and Broden was ready to be free of the constant reminder that his brother no longer lived. 'Twas of no consequence that Broden was responsible for Ewan's early demise. He certainly was not missing any sleep over such a hideous deed. Broden had done what was needed in order for his plans to come to fruition. It was not fair that killing his brother had gained him nothing but to be exiled in his own land and from the clan.

But Gregor was another matter entirely. The boy resembled Ewan so much that 'twas if his brother peered at him from beyond the grave. It had given Broden pause. He had considered killing the boy and yet, somehow, he could never lift the blade that would end his nephew's life. Apparently, somewhere deep inside Broden, he had a conscience after all. Such a revelation surprised him and 'twould certainly shock anyone else who knew him.

Still… the boy had been a pain in his arse from the moment Broden had taken Gregor captive. His constant griping to be returned to his family, for food to fill his belly, or to relieve himself had turned into an hourly, if not by the minute, complaint. Broden had had enough of the child and was more than ready to have him go back to his mother… that is… as long as they paid the ransom.

"I hate ye," Gregor sneered loudly, contempt flashing across his young features. "Ye are no uncle of mine."

"Ye think I care if ye claim me as kin?" Broden gave a wicked chuckle. "I think we are past such a point in our relationship. Ye are only a means for me tae gain monies from the new laird so I may make a life for myself far from these shores."

"Ye could travel tae the ends of the earth and Laird Aiden would still find ye!" Gregor taunted. "That is, if Laird Aiden is feeling merciful and will let ye live for the offense of taking me from my home. Ye will pay for what ye have done!"

"Dunborough should have been mine!" Broden bellowed angrily.

The boy had the nerve to laugh. "The lands and control of the clan was never yers, Uncle, nor would they ever have been even if ye *had* gained control of the keep the night Laird Aiden took over. Ye think tae highly of yerself."

A growl of outrage erupted from Broden. "And ye talk too much, ye damn brat from hell."

"I am certain ye shall learn first-hand how truly hot hell will be, since ye shall be visiting soon, Uncle." The smile on the boy's face was almost Broden's undoing.

"I will be far from here by this time tomorrow. Ye mark my words, Now, shut up," Broden said before stuffing the linen into place and muzzling any further words from the boy.

Finally... blessed silence, although the look Gregor threw him would have felled an entire forest. The boy would kill him if he but had a blade to put into Broden's gut. But no matter. Broden had set into motion something that could not be halted and soon he would have monies aplenty to board a ship and travel wherever the winds would take him.

'Twas a sound plan, he mused, whilst gathering the belt holding his scabbard and placing it around his waist. His blade had been sharpened to the best of his ability while he had been rotting away in this God forsaken hovel. Soon, he would have enough monies to see him properly adorned in clothes and jewels fit for any lord of the realm. He would buy himself land with a castle with servants aplenty to cater to his every whim. All would call him master as he reveled in his newfound wealth and position.

Aye... such was the life he was always meant to live. In charge of all that surrounded him instead of a second son living on the scraps thrown to him by an older brother he despised. His only regret was Iona. She was a loss. He wished he could somehow still capture her unawares, but if she remained inside the castle walls, there was little hope. Any time he had seen her in the village, she had been with the new laird or surrounded by too many knights to overcome. He was an accomplished swordsmen but being out numbered would not gain him much.

The new laird would surely not adhere to Broden's demands that he come alone. Broden would do the same if he were in MacLaren's position. But the given location and the time of day had been part of Broden's plan to grab the monies, turn over the boy, and then make a hasty retreat all before any could come to the laird's aid. Treachery was afoot, he was certain. Treachery on both ends, and Broden decided at the last minute that he would tie Gregor to a tree some distance away to ensure adequate time to escape. What could possibly go wrong?

Everything… had not everything gone wrong the instant Broden had plunged his sword into his brother's back? But there had been no regrets when he had killed Ewan and there certainly would be no regrets that he had now taken his brother's son. He could only move forward with his plan and pray everything played out in his favor.

With no further time to consider a different path than what he had already schemed, Broden hoisted Gregor up, pulling his arm. They made their way to the door and Broden yanked on the handle. The door came partially off its hinges and hung at an odd angle. Broden shrugged and pulled the boy through the portal, not caring for the condition in which he was leaving the hut. He was done with the place. 'Twould be the last time he had to spend another night in such degrading surroundings. Aye! His life would be better as soon as he could rid himself of his nephew and collect all that was due him!

Traipsing through the woods, Broden continued pulling Gregor along to make the boy to adhere to Broden's wishes. It was a pull and push game that he was barely wining as the boy's strength was far greater than Broden had expected. When Gregor began to fight Broden by thrashing around, Broden had had more than enough of the bruises that would be forming on his legs. He was tired of being kicked and screamed at, although the latter at least was not an issue at the moment, thanks to the gag. Still… this was a good a place as any to leave the boy. The location was far enough away from where Broden was to meet MacLaren yet close enough he could get to his nephew in case his plan failed. He refused to think he would not be victorious when this was all said and done.

Once the boy was tied securely to the tree, Broden never looked back. There was no need. He would get his coins and tell Aiden where to find the boy. It would be up to the new laird to find the spot. Broden had had his fill being tortured and kicked by a small boy.

He continued onward as quietly as he could, and saw that Aiden had already arrived at the place they were to meet. 'Twas a well-sized clearing where the trees were far enough away that they would not interfere if it came to a fight. A babbling brook was nearby, with moss covered rocks along its banks. Beneath his feet was either dirt or small shrubbery that should not hinder his getaway. He entered the clearing. His gaze traveling around to see what awaited him in the shadows. It appeared that MacLaren was alone, but Broden knew better.

"Ye surprise me," Broden growled out, whilst fingering the hilt of his sword.

Aiden appeared as though he had not a care in the world and Broden again wondered where his reinforcements were located. "Why? Because I came to meet you as instructed?" Aiden's reply was too casual.

"Ye are alone," Broden responded with a frown, his eyes still searching the nearby trees.

Aiden shrugged. "You took a mere child in order to see your demands were met. Obviously, I would come in order to have the boy returned to his mother."

"I thought for sure the lady would accompany ye," Broden said, hoping for a glimpse of the fair lady.

"Iona is safe at the castle and far from you and any harm you might think to inflict upon her," Aiden answered, looking behind Broden. "Where is the boy?"

"Safe."

A sound left Aiden's lips. "And you expect me to just turn over the ransom on the word of a murderer without seeing that Gregor is well?"

"Ye will have tae take my word that I speak no falsehood," Broden snarled as he advanced a step. "Give me the monies and let us be done with this."

"You must think I am a fool if you really believe I would turn over the monies from my coffers without seeing the boy."

Broden cursed. This should have been so simple. He received the coins he demanded and then he would tell his enemy where he could find his nephew. "Give me what I asked for and then you will learn where I have put Gregor," Broden roared his demand.

Aiden laughed, pulling out his sword from the scabbard at his side. "I think not. We shall finish this together... just you and I."

"This will not gain you the information you need about where I have hidden the boy!" Broden shouted back, whilst reaching for his own blade.

"I have no doubt that I shall indeed find the lady's son with or without your cooperation," Aiden jeered, stepping forward. "A man who would kill his own brother in the back does not have much honor engrained in his soul to keep his word about anything else he might do."

"Ye have no proof," Broden said, whilst his mouth formed a grim line.

"Your stupidity has not gained you anything, you fool. You left a trail with all the proof we need, including Angus's confession of all that you have done. Everything, including Thora's murder, leads straight to you. That you would take your own nephew is the last straw, and I will see you in hell before you harm one more member of this clan," Aiden vowed, holding up his sword.

Broden face flushed with anger as he clenched his teeth. He brought up his blade and stepped forward to meet his fate. He would be done with this part of his life as soon as he killed the adversary before him. Then, and only then, could he start anew somewhere far from here and on distant shores.

"Let us end this," Broden proclaimed, swinging his sword at Aiden who met him blade for blade.

The sound of steel sheering off steel echoed in the small clearing. 'Twas hard for Broden to determine who had the upper hand as they continued to hack away at each other. MacLaren was well trained, but Broden had not spent all these years in his brother's shadow without learning a thing or two about defending himself. Neither gave the other an opportunity to swing a killing blow and after several minutes Broden knew his arm began to weaken from hefting his sword. He was out of practice after hiding out for so many weeks. Not that he would show his enemy that he tired.

MacLaren swung his blade. It flashed briefly in the fading sunlight. Broden winced when the sword sliced across his upper arm and blood began to stream from the wound. A gasp escaped him, followed by a growl of outrage.

"Do you yield?" MacLaren asked with a sly smile across his mouth, causing Broden's anger to rise.

"Nay! I yield ye nothing, ye bloody bastard," Broden angrily bellowed. He began swinging his sword with a determination to chop off MacLaren's head. But no matter how hard he tried, Broden had yet to inflict even the smallest nick on the man before him, whereas Broden now bled from several cuts upon his body. His chest heaved in his attempt to force air into his lungs. He frowned when MacLaren stepped back.

"I see you tire, but we can continue if you still refuse to see reason," MacLaren taunted. He pressed on. "Tell me where you have hidden the boy."

"Never! Not until ye hand over the ransom," Broden said, advancing once again.

"So be it, but never let it be said I did not offer you the chance to yet live," MacLaren said, bringing up his blade again.

MacLaren's attack was relentless, as though he had found a new energy. Yet Broden had some satisfaction when he was finally able to inflict some harm on his enemy in his turn. But this victory was small, because he still battled for his life, swinging his sword using both hands in an attempt to hang onto the smallest measure of hope. A voice rang out in the near distance, causing Broden's heart to lurch in his chest.

"We have the boy, Aiden!"

"Nay!" Broden yelled out, as all his plans crumbled. He brought up his sword yet again, but his aim missed his target and Aiden's blade pierced Broden's chest. He stumbled back until he fell upon the ground.

Aiden came to stand over him then wiped his blade on Broden's tunic before placing his weapon in his scabbard. "I gave you the chance to yield. May your soul rot in hell for the sins you have committed in this life."

Broden's hand went over his chest in an effort to staunch the flow of blood. 'Twas of no use. He had lost everything he had fought so hard to gain. As his last moments of consciousness left him, the Devil's minions came to take his soul down to the fiery pits of hell and Broden of Clan Ferguson knew no more.

# CHAPTER 26

*I*ona stood at the rear of the chapel waiting for the clan to take their seats. It had been several days since Aiden had been true to his word and had returned Gregor safely back to Dunborough She smiled at her memories; weeping tears of joy, gathering her son into her arms, and smothering him with kisses until his protests over being coddled rang in her ears. She had only smiled and once more kissed his brow before allowing him to head to the kitchens to break his fast.

Now Gregor stood next to her in his finest tunic. A small replica of his sire and a reminder that Ewan would always be with her and own a small piece of her heart. After this day, she would now belong to Aiden, and they would start their lives together. She looked forward to what the future would bring.

"Ye love him, mama?" Gregor asked, looking up at her with those dark brown eyes.

"Aye and I hope ye will someday come tae care for Aiden, too," she said, with a smile of encouragement.

"Ye could do worse, I suppose," the boy chuckled at his own joke. "But Laird Aiden has proven his worth and brought honor back tae the clan. I approve of yer choice of husband."

Iona hid a smirk, seeing the seriousness of her son's features. In his own way, he voiced her own thoughts on the man she was to wed. "I am happy ye approve, son. Now, go take yer place up front."

Gregor tugged on her sleeve and crooked his finger. She leaned down and was pleasantly surprised when he placed a kiss upon her cheek. "I love ye, mama," he said quietly.

"I love ye, too, Gregor."

He smiled before leaving her side and she watched him go sit in the front pew whilst Aiden stood impatiently next to the priest. 'Twas time.

She made her way up the aisle of the chapel. Friendly faces shone with happiness and Iona beamed that the clan also approved of her choice to take Aiden as her husband. Her gaze traveled to her lady in waiting, the only person in the room whose scowl silently displayed her displeasure. But Iona would not allow Deirdre to ruin this day. She would deal with the woman at another time. This day belonged to her and Aiden.

Her eyes traveled to her handsome knight, who looked very impatient to make her his wife. His tunic matched her gown right down to the golden threads of embroidery at the neck and cuffs. Whereas Iona's gown displayed golden flowers, Aiden's appeared in an intricate pattern and Iona would be certain to praise the women who had made his matching attire.

She took the arm Aiden offered her and as the priest began

Mass they sat next to Gregor with Aiden's men sitting behind them. The sermon spoke of uniting the clan and letting past hostilities no longer remain in their hearts. But when the priest addressed the blossoming love between Aiden and Iona, she smiled, knowing his words were true. She had loved Aiden almost at first sight, despite him being the enemy to their land. If she could overlook such a beginning, then she prayed their people would too.

The priest asked Iona and Aiden to stand before the clan whilst he bound their lives together for all eternity. A ribbon of green and gold was wound around their clasped hands and the priest at last declared them husband and wife. The clan cheered even whilst the priest frowned that such an uproar was occurring in his chapel. Aiden placed a chaste kiss upon her lips, and they made their way to the altar to sign their marriage documents.

The chapel began to empty as people returned to the great hall to feast and once Iona and Aiden were alone, he grasped her to him in a fierce hug.

"I have never been happier than I am right now, my wife," Aiden whispered in her ear. "I can barely wait until I can make you completely mine."

She gave a laugh and slapped him playfully. "Shhhh! Elsewise, the priest shall scold ye for defiling his chapel with yer thoughts."

"You are my wife now. Surely anything I might say about bedding you is allowed."

"Not in the chapel, Aiden," she teased, "but later!"

"I suppose if I must wait then I will, but know at the first opportunity I will whisk you away to our chamber," Aiden warned, with a roguish grin.

"I look forward tae the moment when we are alone, husband. But first, let us eat and show the clan that all the past is now where it belongs," Iona replied, pulling on his arm so they could make their way to the keep.

Once inside, another loud cheer went up and, before long, wine was being poured and several toasts on their marriage were being made by many of those in attendance. If Iona had any doubt that Aiden would be accepted, then such thoughts no longer existed. He was her husband and she, his wife. The conquering enemy was now the hero of the clan, especially after killing Broden and returning Gregor back into the fold.

A trencher was put before them, and Aiden selected the choicest of meats for Iona to pick from. They laughed, they drank, and when they had eaten their fill, the tables were cleared so the dancing could begin. With a motion of his hand to the minstrels, Aiden took her hand and led her to the middle of the hall where they began the patterns of a dance. Soon, other couples joined them, and the merriment continued while members of the clan began to ask to dance with their laird or his lady.

It had been some time that Dunborough Castle had seen such entertainment. Yet one look at Aiden, and Iona was more than ready to make her way to their bedchamber. She excused herself, gathered several ladies and they made their way up the turret steps. Deidre stood outside the laird's door.

Iona could tell from the woman's expression that she had much on her mind. "Go enjoy the festivities, Dierdre. I have enough help tae ready myself tae receive my husband," Iona said, whilst her hand took hold of the latch.

"But, my lady," Deirdre began.

Iona peered over her shoulder. "We shall talk on the morrow. Good eve tae ye, Deirdre," she said, dismissing the woman who frowned and at last took her leave.

"Damn uppity and a pain in our arse," one woman swore before her eyes widened. "Me apologies, milady."

Iona patted the woman's hand. "No need and I certainly understand yer concerns. But I shall worry over my lady in waiting another day. Help me from this gown, please."

With the women's help, Iona was changed from her wedding attire to a soft linen. A dark blue robe was just being placed on her shoulders and Iona was in the process of tying the matching sash when the bedchamber door opened whilst her husband filled the space.

Stepping inside, he held the door open in a silent request for the women to leave. They giggled as they filed past him. Shutting the door, he slid the bolt into place. His attention returned to her whilst his eyes smoldered—she assumed in anticipation of their coupling.

Making her way to a small table by the fire set between two comfortable chairs, she took up the pitcher of wine and poured the beverage into a chalice. She raised the cup to her lips and took a sip of the heady wine before holding it out to her husband. "Wine?" she asked, in a soft whisper.

He came to her like an animal stalking its prey. Those crazy hypnotic violet eyes never left hers as he took the cup from her hand, placing the chalice back on the table. He began untying the sash at her waist. "I have other ideas in mind than drinking, my love," he said in a husky tone, pushing the robe from her shoulders. "I have waited long enough to finally make you mine.

"Our wait is at last over," Iona said as she wound her arms around his neck. "Ye belong tae me now and for all time."

He crushed his lips to hers and she heard his moan before he lifted her in his strong arms and carried her to their bed. Clothes were torn from their bodies landing in a heap on the floor. The coverlet was whipped from the bed and Iona scooted across the mattress to make room for her husband. He sat on the edge whilst taking off a boot, tossing it to land next to their clothes with a heavy thud.

Iona knelt and molded herself to his back whilst he worked on the second boot. "How I want ye, my dearest love," she whispered in his ear before giving the lobe a gentle nibble. She heard his laughter rumble deep in his chest.

"My lady wishes to play," he said. He swiftly turned capturing her in his arms and then laying her down beneath him.

She began running her fingers through his red hair, the color so much like her own only shorter. "Aye. All night if ye so wish it, my laird."

His face grew serious as his hand caressed her hair then her cheek. "What a treasure you are, my lovely wife. I never thought I would find you."

"I am happy we found each other, husband. Now make me yours in all ways possible," she commanded, reaching up around his neck. She put the slightest pressure at the base, and he bent forward so their lips could once again meet.

Their mouths joined together, much like their bodies a short while later. Two souls each finding the one destined for the other since the beginning of time itself. And when they found their release together, husband and wife called out each other names. The heavens smiled. They were now together. They were one.

# CHAPTER 27

*T*hey had a fortnight of heavenly bliss before the world intruded on the paradise that Aiden tried to create for his new bride. One whole fortnight before his old life came back to haunt him. They could not dismiss the missive delivered by one of King Henry's messengers. Aiden was expected to travel down to Bamburgh Castle where he was to board a ship to France to fight a war in the king's name. Aiden wanted no part of such a mission. His heart just was not in it.

One of Iona's hands was tucked into the elbow of his arm. She held on tightly whilst peering over his shoulder as he read the missive again. 'Twas a grim reminder of the life he had led in service to a king and the reason he had taken this land in the first place.

"I am to journey south with as many reinforcements as I can bring so I can join his forces in France," Aiden said angrily. "He cares not that I leave this land unprotected if I were to supply him with the entire garrison!" He threw the parchment onto this desk before folding Iona into his arms.

"He canna do that," Iona protested, whilst her head went to rest upon Aiden's chest.

He stroked her hair, offering what comfort he could. "Aye, he can. He is the King of England. I am his vassal. He has snapped his fingers and I am now expected to obey his orders," Aiden said, frowning. He had been torn for some time, his allegiance to England and its king warring with his Scots heritage. He had a stronger call on his allegiance now. He had a family and a clan to protect. Going off to fight in France for King Henry's war with his sons hardly felt justifiable. 'Twas a foolish cause, designed merely to further the king's dominance over his sons. Aiden had been summoned. How could he go against his king?

Iona reached over to retrieve the missive. She scanned it for several minutes, then gazed up into his eyes. "Sons again fighting tae gain control of land and the monarchy. 'Twas futile once before, years ago. What makes them think they will win against their sire this time?"

He placed a kiss on her forehead. "'Tis a quest bound to fail, and his sons should know they will not win against their father."

"What are we going tae do?"

His brow rose as he looked down upon her. "We, my dear, are not going to do anything. You are going to remain here and take care of Gregor and the clan," he answered far more calmly than he felt. He had little choice in the matter, or did he?

"And what are ye planning tae do?" she asked quietly.

"Do you trust me?"

She widened her eyes at his question. "Ye have to ask?"

"Do you trust me?" he repeated waiting for her answer.

"Ye know I trust ye with my life, my love," she said, giving him what he could only term a weak smile.

"I cannot in good conscience serve an English King any longer, but must align myself with King William. 'Twill be considered treason to those I once served. I will no longer be able to step on English soil again and risk being taken by our enemies."

"Are ye sure ye wish tae do this? Yer family home is on English soil. How will ye possibly not see yer family again? Yer sister is yer twin, Aiden. Such a bond is hard tae ignore," she stated, clutching his tunic.

He placed his lips on hers and kissed her. "'Tis true Berwyck Castle has been my home and would have been mine to govern. But that all changed when my sister's husband laid siege to the place. I have not called Berwyck home in many a year and 'tis why I have wandered both England and France trying to find my place in life. I took this assignment so that I would finally be able to call a place home and then I found you." He smiled down, staring into her eyes.

She nodded. "I may have hated ye when ye first captured Dunborough, but I am glad now that ye did."

"I will ride come the morn for Berwyck so that I may let Amir know of my decision to remain on Scottish soil and serve King William," he declared. "She will understand and know my visits to Berwyck from this point forward will be limited or scarce."

She cupped the palm of her hand to his cheek. "I could go with ye."

"Absolutely not."

"But Aiden…"

He took both her cheeks in his hands and quickly kissed her. "My lady love… as much as I desire for you to be by my side, to travel the world if that is your wish, I cannot allow you to follow me to Berwyck, at least not at this time. Surely you understand why you must needs remain here."

Her sigh was heavy, much like Aiden's own conscience. He had brought this war to their doorstep by invading this land in the first place. Now he needed to end this and ensure they would be safe from a grasping king.

She finally found her voice. "I will miss ye."

"As I will miss you and Gregor. I promise someday I will take ye to Berwyck to meet my family, as long as I can ensure our safety. There is much to tell you about the place of my birth, but I will save that for another time."

"We could always visit yer younger sister and her family up at Urquhart," she murmured softly. "I am certain Lynet and Ian would welcome us into their home."

"Aye. They are safe on Scottish soil. I promise you shall meet all my siblings, Iona. I am proud to call you my wife and Gregor my son. All shall eventually work itself out. And who knows… mayhap Berwyck will one day be conquered by a Scottish King. Such has happened before over the centuries. Anything is possible."

"'Tis an important stronghold on our borders. I doubt England would relinquish such a fortress easily."

"Aye and my sister's husband was not called the Devil's Dragon for nothing. We shall worry about the ownership of Berwyck another day. For now, help me pack a few things for my journey. I will take only Finlay with me and leave the rest of my guards here to protect you."

Iona's brow furrowed. "What if another runner from the king appears in yer absence?"

"Anyone arriving can be told I am not here. There are plenty of knights here to guard you and, with our home on an island, you will be safe." Aiden took her hand and began leading her to their bedchamber.

"And the knight who sent the king's missive?" she asked, whilst they walked down the passageway.

"I will send him on his way come the morn. Since he has delivered his message, I am certain he has others and will need to travel quickly," Aiden replied as he opened the door for his wife to enter their room. She strode past him, caressing his tunic with her fingertips and sending him a promising look over her shoulder.

"Bolt the door, my love," she ordered with a wistful smile.

Aiden gave a light chuckle before doing as she commanded. The afternoon became all the brighter as he pleasured his wife until she was completely satisfied.

# CHAPTER 28

*I*ona left her bedchamber and continued down the passageway to the turret. Carefully descending the curved stairs, she came into the great hall. 'Twas later in the morn than the time she normally came down to break her fast but, with Aiden gone, she had had a restless night. Sleep had evaded her, and she tossed and turned the night away until she at last found her slumber close to dawn.

Looking around the empty hall, she saw she was alone. How unusual. Normally there was at least a servant busily going about cleaning the place up after the morning meal. But there was no one and an eerie silence caused her to shiver. Where was everyone?

She crossed the room to the back where the kitchen was located, and peered inside. A pot boiled over onto what was left of the fire and Iona quickly grabbed a cloth so she could swing the lever the pot hung on. Cook must have left in a hurry, and it was strange that he would leave his kitchen unattended. Iona frowned, seeing the ingredients for the afternoon meal on the table, still waiting to be prepared. Something was not right.

A curse came from outside in the garden and Iona felt a sliver of relief knowing someone was outside. She saw Deidre calmly sitting on the stone bench, her back resting on the wall behind her.

"Finally," she sneered. "I was beginning tae think I would need tae wake yer lazy arse from yer slumber."

Iona came to a halt at the woman's words. "Excuse me?"

"Ye could have been more accommodating tae my plans and woken earlier, ye stupid chit," Deidre answered, coming to a stand.

'Twas then that Iona smelled a distant fire, most likely in the village. That would certainly take every available person out of the castle to assist with putting it out before it could spread.

"Ye set a fire?" Iona asked. Deidre nodded. "But why?"

A snort left the woman. "Why? Ye were never very bright, Iona. Did ye not think I would want revenge against those who killed my kin?"

Iona wracked her brain until the connection was at last made. How could she have ever forgotten that Deidre was a distant cousin to Ewan and Broden? But their relationship was so scarce that Iona never thought Deidre would ever side with Iona's brother-in-law. Why would she?

"Ye were loyal tae Broden," Iona stated with a frown.

"Of course, I was loyal tae Broden!" Her voice screeched and echoed into the distance. "He was the son I never had whilst Ewan only treated me like a servant. Making me lady in waiting tae ye was an insult, when I should have been lady of the keep."

Iona frowned. "How could ye possibly be lady of the hall,

Deidre, when Ewan was the heir and leader of the clan?" Iona asked, knowing the woman's statement was irrational. Ewan had inherited everything, including his title, which was held by his father before him. Gregor would have one day inherited the responsibility if Aiden had not taken over.

"Details... details... they dinnae matter, only that I should have been the lady here and not ye," Deidre screamed. Her face became distorted in her rage. She raised her fist to the heavens as though cursing her fate. The woman clearly was mad, but then she turned her crazed eyes in Iona's direction. This woman had a plan for her and Iona did not wish to learn what it was.

She turned to flee but was stopped by a tall stranger who swung his arm in Iona's direction. She tried to duck, but something solid hit her head and Iona fell to the ground. Deidre cackled in glee whilst Iona lay there, stunned. Deidre had some evil purpose in mind and was willing to do whatever it took to see her desires were met.

Deidre towered over Iona, who screamed until a rag was shoved into her mouth so she could no longer protest what was happening to her. Iona tried to focus, but the man who had hit her had done his job for her head seemed to reel, her stomach lurched and the two people bending over her seemed to have ghost shadows, as if they were dividing into two.

"There. Finally silence from ye so, I no longer have tae hear yer pitiful voice," Deidre said in apparent satisfaction. She pointed to the man hovering nearby. "Pick her up and let us finish this."

The man hesitated. "Ye never said I had tae do more than hit the woman. This will cost ye extra," he said folding his arms across his chest.

Deidre swore and then reached into the pouch held by a string at her waist. She held out several coins and tossed them to the man. "Now, ye have been paid. Pick her up and follow me."

Iona's head swam as she was hoisted none to gently over the man's shoulder. He swung her around to go back into the castle. Her hair was pulled up and Iona stared into the crazed eyes of Deidre.

"Yer new living quarters await ye, dear Iona.," she sneered, before letting go of her hair and walking around her captor.

Iona's eyes widened when they went into the kitchen and through the doorway leading down into the depths of Dunborough. *Nay! Not the dungeon.* No help would come from above if they had no knowledge that she was down here and as far as Iona knew, the cells were completely empty. Iona swung her arms at the man's back but 'twas of no use. Her mind might be telling her to fight but her body could do nothing whilst her head was injured. She was doing everything in her power not to pass out.

They continued their way down into the bowels of the castle. Once on the level of the cells, Deidre took hold of one of the torches held in a wall sconce. They continued onward into the back portion of the dungeon. 'Twas dark and no light from the main room lit this place, since they rarely used these cells.

Iona was dropped inside and a loud clank echoed when the bars shut behind her. She did her best to sit up on the filthy floor and quickly scanned her surroundings. A rat scurried from a mattress that appeared as though it had been here since the beginning of time. A wooden bucket sat next to a stool that looked as if it would crack if anyone chanced to sit upon it. All in all, 'twas not a place any human being would want to reside. And once the torch was gone that Deidre held, Iona would be in complete darkness.

"Enjoy yer new chambers, Iona. Mayhap I may even remember tae feed ye... or maybe I will not..." Deidre said, chuckling. She turned her attention to the man next to her. "What are ye still doing here? Go! Yer job is done, ye have been amply paid, and yer services are no longer needed." Diedre turned the lock with a key on a string that disappeared beneath her gown and then left.

The light from the torch disappeared with the pair and Iona was plunged into complete darkness. A rat ran over her legs and a weak scream left her lips. Her head pounded. Iona reached up to feel a growing bump and blood upon her fingers. She knew once she was coherent, she would need to come up with some sort of plan so she could escape, although she knew not what. Her situation was grim, and Aiden was too far away to be of any help. Who would come to her aid now? And with that final thought, Iona passed out cold.

# CHAPTER 29

Aiden halted his horse on the beach whilst Finlay did the same. Staring off into the distance, he gave a heavy sigh of contentment. *Home!* The sight of Berwyck Castle sitting on the distant hill almost brought tears to his eyes. How long had it been since he had entered the great hall? Seen his family and niece and nephew? 'Twas clear too much time had passed, and guilt swept over him for not coming home sooner.

A quick glance at Finlay showed Aiden his friend was feeling as nostalgic with the castle at last in sight. They would surely be just as overwhelmed once they passed under its barbican gate and entered the keep. Aiden nodded toward Finlay, who returned the gesture. No words were necessary as they put their horses into a gallop to reach the castle as quickly as their horses would carry them.

The horses thundered over the beach, causing clumps of sand to fly off behind them. They crossed the river and went into the trees at a slower pace as they began the climb to the higher elevation. Soon, their steeds clip clopped over the wooden bridge whilst knights on the battlement walls above called out their greetings to the weary travelers. 'Twould be good to have the ground beneath their feet and to find comfort in a goblet of mead and food to fill their bellies.

Word spread rapidly of Aiden's arrival and soon a small crowd had gathered in the inner bailey to welcome them. Jumping from his saddle, he saw his sister leaving the keep with her two children at her side. With their deep black hair, there was no mistaking who their sire was. She leaned down to the boy and whispered in his ear before the lad of eight summers went down the stairs and came to stand before him. He gave his uncle a short bow.

"Welcome home, Uncle," Royce proclaimed. "We have been expecting you."

"You have?" Aiden asked pondering how they could have known of his arrival.

"Mother has been hoping for your return for many a year now." He crossed his arms over his chest much like his father Dristan had done, and Aiden tried not to laugh at the boy's copy of his sire.

"I see. Well, young Royce, I am home now for a brief visit. Lead the way back to your mother," Aiden said, whilst his gaze took in the crowd. Finlay was also being welcomed by several of the MacLaren clan and was being whisked away. As for himself, a man whom he had thought of as an uncle came to stand before him to pull Aiden into his arms for a fierce embrace.

A rumbled harrumph left Killian when he finally let go. "It took ye long enough for yer feet tae finally make yer way home," he grumbled. "What took ye so long?"

"'Tis a long story and best told behind closed doors. Has all been well here?" Aiden asked. Lady Ella came to join the man before him. Killian took the lady's hand and brought it up to his lips. Aiden lifted one brow and gave the couple an amused look.

"My wife," Killian announced, with a sly grin.

"'Tis long past due," Aiden said before bowing. "My lady…"

Ella swatted his arm. "Enough of that," she chided. "That title no longer is necessary when addressing me… as if 'twas ever needed."

"Aiden!" Amiria called, waving to him once her son rejoined her.

Aiden smiled. "I best not keep her waiting any longer."

Killian laughed. "Nothing has changed on that account. 'Tis good to have you home, Aiden."

Ella went to him, stood on the tips of her toes, and kissed his cheek. "Aye. Your sister will be happy about your return."

Aiden nodded to the couple before making his way up the steps to the keep. He bowed to his sister but once he rose, she wrapped her arms around him. A small sob escaped her, and he held her at arms-length.

"Tears for me, dearest sister?" He asked with a cocky grin.

Amiria turned away to wipe the moisture from her eyes. "I admit to nothing," she replied before turning back to him. "I am certain you remember Royce who just greeted you. Liliana was only a babe the last time you were here."

Aiden gazed at his sister's children whilst Liliana went to

hide behind her mother. His heart lurched in his chest with regret that he was not closer to his own nephew and niece but there was no way to change the past nor what lay in his future.

"I have much to discuss with you," Aiden said, looking into the same violet eyes as his own.

"Why do I have the notion this visit will be short?" she asked, linking her arm through his.

He did not reply, for his words would only cause her sorrow, and if she were to shed any more tears, she would do so behind a closed door. They entered the keep and Aiden had to stop for a moment to take in the overwhelming feeling that this may be the last time he ever entered this hall again.

Memories rushed across his mind in a flurry, reminding him of what this place had meant to him. 'Twas to be his birthright, but that all changed one day during the siege of 1174 when Dristan, the Devil's Dragon of Blackmore, invaded their home. He remembered little of the fighting, except being struck down next to their sire and being whisked away until he could recover enough to return. His sister had thought him dead all those months. Instead, Aiden had come home to find her happily married to the very enemy who had taken everything from him.

"Aiden?"

Hearing his name whispered from his sister brought him out of his sudden melancholy mood. There was no sense dredging up the past. His future was not here within these walls but with a lady he longed to return to along the Scottish shore.

"Where is Dristan?" he asked, instead of continuing to relive memories that would do him no good.

"Summoned to Bamburgh to attend the king," she answered,

after giving over the care of the children to one of her ladies in waiting. After walking through the great hall, they entered one of the turrets leading to the upper floors where the family had their chambers. "I expect his return any day now. Is this why you are also here? Passing through on your way south?"

"Nay 'tis of another nature, but let us get behind closed doors before we have speech together," he replied, as they continued down the passageway on the fourth floor.

Amiria stopped at his chamber door... or what used to be his bedchamber that is. She opened the portal and stepped inside whilst he followed directly behind her. He halted mid-step whilst his eyes wandered from one corner of the bedchamber to the other. 'Twas as though he had been here but yestereve, as everything was still in place as he had left it.

Amiria smiled at his reaction and went to stand near a set of chairs near the hearth that had yet to be lit. "As you can see, we left your things here for when you returned."

"How did you know I would?" he asked, coming to stand opposite her.

She reached for his hands. "I had hope and never gave up that one day you would walk through Berwyck's gates again."

"'Tis a short trip, sister," he replied with a heavy sigh.

"'Tis clear you have much on your mind. Come... tell me all so I can ease your troubles, for I can see that the matter weighs heavily on your mind."

He squeezed her hands, before letting go as she took a seat in one of the chairs. He undid the buckle of his belt holding his scabbard and sword, setting the weapon up against the wall before sitting to face his sister.

"I have wed," he began until she interrupted him.

"What?"

"Aye. You will love her and her son," Aiden said, whilst holding up his hand to halt the reprimand he knew was to come. "I know I should have waited until you and Dristan were present, but I was pressed for time. As I said, there is much to tell you."

"Father Donovan will be distressed he did not perform the ceremony himself," she declared with a frown.

"He yet lives?" he asked, thinking the priest must be ancient by now.

She gave a light laugh. "He is getting on in years but aye, he yet lives."

His sister continued gazing upon him with a quizzical brow. "Do you love her?"

Aiden gave a small chuckle. "I would not have wed her if I did not. Surely you know that much about me."

Amiria shrugged. "To be honest, you have been gone so long 'tis hard to say what I know about you these days, brother. We may be twins, but we have also been known to disagree on many an occasion in our past."

He nodded at her comment. "Fair enough. Let me begin from when I last saw you…"

His telling of the past several years caused Amiria to laugh in all the right places, gasp out when he told her of several situations where he could have died, and finally he confessed all that had occurred at Dunborough and his possible position of turning to serve a Scottish king.

"So, you can see my dilemma," he finally stated, after he had laid his heart out at the feet of his sibling. He knew that Amiria would understand more than any other, considering she was his twin. But mayhap the years apart had also taken away the connection that they had always shared.

"King Henry will consider this an act of treason no matter what happens with his war in France against his own kin," she stated, whilst her fingers drummed on the wooden arms of the chair.

"Aye… hence harboring me within these very walls could be considered an act of treason when the king would as soon see me in his dungeon's pit."

Amiria shuddered. "Let us not think on something so drastic yet. You must rest from your trip, and we shall speak with Dristan upon his return."

"'Tis not wise for me to be here too long, Amiria. I had hoped to quietly come to see you and the children and then leave as silently as I had arrived," he answered, with a worried frown set upon his face.

"If that had been your desire, then you should have entered Berwyck from the hidden passageway instead of our front gates. Word will spread quickly, and before long every MacLaren clan member will be here to help celebrate your return."

His eyes became wide in panic. "I will not put you in danger."

She waved her hands as though she had not a worry in the world. "Nonsense. 'Twill not come to that. Now take your ease and know you are safe here in your home. I will see you at the evening meal."

Amiria rose from her chair and came over to kiss his cheek.

"I have missed you, brother," she whispered before taking her leave.

With the closing of the door, Aiden took a deep breath to calm his racing heart. He was home and home had never felt this good.

# CHAPTER 30

*I*ona awoke with a start, shivering in the sheer darkness of her cell where she could not even see her hand in front of her face. Remnants of her dream shook her to her core, leaving her with a dismal sense that no help would be arriving soon. She sat up, leaning against the cold stones at her back whilst the image of Ewan cursing her from her dream echoed in her mind. *'Twas but a nightmare... he would wish for me to be happy.* Still... she continued to be plagued by the words in the dream Ewan spoke about how she had betrayed him and their clan by falling in love with their enemy. She could not help where her heart had led her, and she would not forsake the love she bore for Aiden.

"Aiden... where are you, my love?"

There was no answer to her heartfelt plea. Her husband did not miraculously appear and sweep her from this God-forsaken dungeon of despair. How long had she been here? Days? A se'n-night mayhap more? She had no sense of time and yet she had to remain strong, not only for herself but her son. Only God above knew what Deidre had in store for Gregor.

She had to get out of here. Although Iona could now see clearly again, her head still ached. When she could finally stand, she had gone to the bars of the cell and rattled them until her fingers hurt. Calling for aid got her nothing except a raw throat. She had finally given up hoping that anyone above would hear her. She would have thought that, at the very least, Aiden's friends would be searching for her, but how was she to know what was happening above? 'Twas hopeless...

But she had her faith... faith in God and faith that Aiden would return and find her. 'Twas the only thing that had been keeping her sane. She fell to her knees and began to pray as she had done every day since her captivity. Surely her petitions to God would be heard today. If not, she would continue to lift them up to the heavens until they were answered.

Time once more stood still in the musty cell that was now her home. Her stomach rumbled in hunger. Her mouth parched from lack of water beyond the rivulet that occasionally ran down the wall, perhaps when it rained beyond the castle. She had found it when she put a hand to that part of the wall, and it came away wet. It was all that sustained her. No other sustenance appeared to be forthcoming, and Iona feared she would waste away to nothing before anyone would find her. A sob escaped her as she continued to bemoan her plight. Why would God not answer her? She refused to give up hope. She prayed to God on Aiden's behalf. Prayed that God would keep him safe, and he would return home to Dunborough soon. Tears raced down her cheeks with worry for her husband and son.

*Aiden... where are you, my love?*

Aiden lifted his head from his meal and quickly scanned the room He could swear he had heard Iona's voice in the crowded hall. 'Twas but a whisper, but still he felt her presence as though she was near. Perchance 'twas a sign. One he should take to heart. He had already told Amiria that he had been at Berwyck far longer than intended, but she had insisted Aiden wait for Dristan's return. He had waited nigh unto six days. Six days! Days when he should have been riding north to ensure his family and clan's safety instead of feasting and making merry. 'Twas certain that the MacLaren clan knew how to welcome home their prodigal son.

He raised his goblet to his lips and drank the heady red wine. Amiria sat to his left. The trencher they had shared still contained some food but since she sat back in her chair, Aiden assumed she had eaten her fill. To his right sat his younger sister Sabina. She still had not revealed all her story, only that she had been spending most of her days at Haversham Abby, although she had never taken her final vows as a nun. Aiden assumed that the good sisters allowed her to live among them because of the monies Dristan continued to gift them. He shuddered at the thought of living a life of chastity. He could not imagine any sister of his devoting her life to God, but that would be up to Sabina.

He took hold of Sabina's hand and she gazed at him with soft brown eyes. She returned to her meal and once more, Aiden wondered at the horrors that her sister had endured years ago. Amiria would not tell him, and it appeared Sabina did not wish to relive the memories either. She had become very tight-lipped, only speaking when spoken to. Perchance some of that could be laid at Aiden's feet. He had not been kind to this particular sibling in his youth and he prayed Sabina would one day forgive him.

He turned in his chair and was about to voice his thoughts when the keep's door opened, and a loud cheer arose in the great hall. A small contingent of men entered, whipping off their rain-drenched dark red capes. Their black tunics emblazed with a golden dragon proved they were the men of Dristan of Berwyck, and there was the man himself, making his way to his wife. Amiria rose from her chair and began running toward him and when she reached Dristan, he lifted her high in the air. Her laughter filled the room until she was brought back down, and Dristan bent forward to kiss her lips. Another cheer went up and knights and ladies raised their chalices to toast their returning lord.

Toward the rear of the knights who made their way to several tables was a young man and Aiden could scarcely believe his eyes. His younger brother Patrick made his way to the raised dais, bowed before Sabina, and then was pulled into her embrace. Patrick widened his eyes when he espied Aiden sitting next to the woman who refused to let him go, and Patrick gave Aiden a wink. The young scamp.

"Here now, Sabina, let the young man go before he has no energy to give his favorite brother a fond hello," Aiden teased whilst watching Sabina laugh for the first time.

"Of course," she said with a bright smile. "So many years have slowly passed by since we have seen him last. Almost as long as you, Aiden."

Patrick gave Aiden a quick hug. "Hello, brother. The years apart have been long, have they not?"

"Long enough for you to become a man, it appears," Aiden said, looking the boy over. Patrick was about to take a seat next to Sabina, but she quickly stood.

"Nay, Patrick. Sit next to Aiden. I am certain you have much to have speech about and you must needs eat your fill," she ordered, moving to the next seat down.

"My thanks, sister," Patrick replied. He turned his attention to the food spread before him. A clean trencher was given to him by an ever-efficient servant, and he began to fill it with various meats. Soon he was stuffing his mouth as though the food was going to be taken from him. He finally looked up at Aiden, who continued to stare upon him. "What?"

"You have grown," Aiden stated the obvious. "Where is Riorden de Deveraux? Are you still serving him?"

Patrick shook his head and then pointed toward Dristan, who was attempting to take his place at the table but continued to be halted by several clansmen. "Riorden released me whilst at Bamburgh. Said 'twas time I returned to Berwyck and Dristan's care. He said there was nothing further he could teach me, but I would learn much by returning home."

"I must do the same... return home that is," Aiden replied with a worried frown. He could feel something in his gut that told him he must needs return to Dunborough, and quickly.

"Are you not home already, brother?" Patrick asked, halting his fork as it rose to his mouth.

"Only for a short visit, and I have already stayed longer than I should have."

"I am sure the family will adjourn to Dristan's solar after we have eaten our fill. There is much news to share," Patrick said and then began eating his fill once more.

Dristan at last made it to his place at the table. He reached over to Aiden and clasped his arm in a hearty welcome. He reached for his goblet that a servant had just filled with wine and raised his cup in a toast.

"To our family that is once more reunited," Dristan proclaimed, as he looked upon the MacLaren siblings.

Another loud chorus of *hear hears* echoed in the great hall. Dristan sat and began filling his trencher much as Patrick had done. After he had eaten his fill, he asked his wife and her siblings to join him in his solar. They all made their way upstairs and the door was shut behind Patrick who entered last.

"We have spent far too many years apart and even longer it seems since we have all been together in the same room," Dristan stated, looking around the room.

"'Twould make everything complete if only Lynet and Ian were here," Amiria said, clearly upset they were missing their sister and her husband.

Aiden went to Amiria and gave her hand a squeeze. "'Tis a long way for her to come for a visit but mayhap you shall see her soon."

Sabina took one of the vacant chairs. "Tell us about the news from Bamburgh, Dristan. We have been dying of curiosity since you left."

Dristan took a chair by the hearth and pulled his wife into his lap, not caring that others witnessed such an open display of affection. "To be honest, I had not thought I would be home this soon. I thought for certain I would be boarding a ship for France."

Amiria ran her hand over his black hair before resting it upon his cheek. "I am most thankful you are home."

Dristan took her hand and kissed it. "Needless to say, King Henry has no need of my immediate services, although, as you know, that could change. The rebellion between the king and his sons, Young Henry and Richard, is at an end after the king learned his heir died of a fever."

"Young Henry is dead?" Aiden asked with wide eyes.

"Aye," Dristan answered, continuing. "The king plans to name Richard his heir, although I highly doubt Richard will gain any power until the death of his father. There are other rumors floating around court as to what will happen with Aquitaine, but I cared not to listen to idle gossip. The king informed me I could return to Berwyck, and I left as soon as I was given leave to do so, bringing Patrick home with me."

"I am surprised Riorden did not join you," Aiden commented, knowing how close the two men were.

"He was just as anxious to return to his wife as I to return to mine. We wasted little time with pleasantries other than releasing Patrick from his oath of fealty to the man he served these many years." Dristan turned his attention to Aiden. "Amiria told me whilst I supped that you are now wed and hold Dunborough in King Henry's name. Are you certain you do not wish to hold it instead for the Scottish king?"

Aiden's eyes went wide that the couple had held such a conversation over their dinner, but it certainly sped up lengthy conversations when all he wanted was to also return to his home. "My sister knows me well. I only wanted to come here to let you know of my decision to remain in Scotland and be loyal to their king since I am now in charge of the Ferguson Clan."

"You shall be considered a traitor!" Patrick yelled out in anger whilst bolting from his chair.

Dristan held up his hand and Patrick returned to his seat. "Aiden will no more be considered a traitor within these halls than Lynet and Ian. They are family and family will always be welcome here at Berwyck."

Amiria turned to face Aiden whilst tears began forming in her eyes. "We will miss you, Aiden."

"Tears for me again, Amiria?" Aiden teased.

"'Tis this pregnancy that makes me so melancholy. I blame Dristan," she huffed, crossing her arms over her chest even whilst Dristan laughed.

"I shall gladly accept any and all blame for my dearest wife's current state of mind," he chuckled, and began whispering in her ear. Amiria blushed and Aiden could only ponder what had caused her to do so.

They spent the rest of the evening speaking of things that had occurred over the years, each sibling telling their own story in their own way. And when Aiden went to his bedchamber that night, his heart was full of peace knowing his family here at Berwyck was in good hands. With the dawn, Aiden and Finlay left Berwyck and headed north toward home and the new life that awaited them at Dunborough Castle.

# CHAPTER 31

*I*ona clutched the threadbare blanket around her, trying to retain whatever warmth her body still had. She was trembling from the cold and starving. 'Twas no way anyone should die, but she had peace with the knowledge that she would meet the good Lord above soon. She was forgotten in this hellhole. No one had come to save her, and she was beyond the point of saving herself. She just didn't have the strength to fight anymore.

A flash of light brought her out of her daze, and she had a hard time adjusting her eyes to the brightness. Was it real or just a figure of her imagination? At this point in her imprisonment, 'twas hard to tell. She had given up hope days ago... or was it weeks? In the darkness, she had lost any sense of how much time had passed her by.

The bars to her cell swung open and a bowl of what only could be termed gruel was set down next to her. A cackle of glee left her captor's lips. Iona could only wish she had the energy to fight her tormentor.

"Come tae gloat, Diedre?" Iona asked in a meek tone through cracked lips. Her eyes attempted to focus once again to see if this woman thought to bring her water, but Diedre's hands were empty. Iona supposed she should be thankful the woman brought whatever slop was to serve as nourishment.

"'Tis no sense in gloating when ye are not up tae the task of verbally sparing with me, Iona," her enemy chuckled, rubbing her hands together. "And just in case ye are interested, no one misses ye above. 'Tis as though ye never existed."

Iona did not take the bait, though she could not believe that not even a single person was searching for her. It made no sense for the clan to forget their lady. Her hands trembled as she reached for the bowl, and she scooped the food into her mouth with the spoon. She tried not to gag. This was not even fit for the pigs! But since this was the only bit of food she would apparently get, she consumed the gruel all the same. She could only hope the food would somehow give her strength to fight this woman the next time she returned.

Once finished, she set the bowl down and pulled the blanket over her shoulders. Diedre continued to stare down at her whilst standing by the door.

"What have ye done with Gregor?" Iona finally asked. Worry about what this woman would do to her son consumed her.

Diedre's laughter filled her head as it echoed off the walls of the dungeon. "I will mold him into the kind of laird Dunborough needs. He is young. He will forget ye soon enough."

"A child never forgets their mother, Diedre. If you had children of yer own, ye would know this for yerself," Iona whispered but 'twas the wrong thing to say as the woman screeched out in anger.

"Ye know nothing of what I have suffered in my lifetime! The humiliation! Being an outcast!" Diedre bellowed, and then began mumbling to herself as a distant sound caused her to halt her speech. "Nay! It cannae be!"

Before Iona could even begin to understand what was happening, the space outside of her cell was filled with torchlight and she shielded her eyes from the brightness. Her knights had come to her rescue and Aiden was leading the way. He shoved passed Diedre to reach Iona. She sobbed in relief as she lifted her hands around his neck.

"Ye came for me," she cried out, whilst her husband's arms protectively wrapped themselves around her, helping her to stand.

"Of course, I came for you. With a little help from our son," Aiden replied, looking toward the small boy who pushed his way through his clansmen to reach his mother.

"I told ye Lady Diedre was up tae something, father," Gregor said, standing there with a triumphant look that said he had been right all along. Iona and Aiden's brow rose at one word in what he had said.

"What?" the boy asked, his gaze shifting between them.

Aiden placed his arm around Gregor as he continued to steady Iona in place. "You called me father."

Gregor shrugged. "I suppose ye will be around for a long while and ye did marry my mother, after all."

Iona could barely contain her joy that Gregor was safe. "How did you know were tae find me?" she asked softly.

Gregor pointed to Diedre. "That one tried tae keep me

locked up in my bedchamber but I escaped her and hid where she could not find me. I have been watching her for days. When she made her way down to the dungeon, I ran tae tell Laird Aiden, knowing most ladies would not wish to go into the castle depths," he replied, with a satisfied grin.

Aiden kissed her brow. "I returned days ago only to learn you had gone missing. Diedre tried to tell all that you had merely run away. I knew this was a falsehood, as did the clan. Logan, Colin, Duncan, and Gavin were beside themselves with worry and had already sent out scouts to every village within miles of Dunborough. 'Tis a good thing they had already put a search into motion, or I would have been a madman and most likely challenged them to defend themselves, since I put you in their care."

The men mumbled their apologies and Iona could only forgive them. 'Twas not their fault she had been taken. Diedre had planned everything very well, despite failing in the end. Iona's gaze fell on the woman who had served her. Her eyes were glazed over, and clearly, she was not of a right mind.

Aiden began helping Iona from the cell and called over his shoulder. "Put Diedre in the cell and give her a taste of how my wife felt being held captive in the dark."

"Nay!" Diedre moaned in agony, as guards came to take the woman's arms and pull her in the direction of the cell.

"Wait!" Iona halted their progress to the stairs that would lead her from this horrible place. She turned to her husband. "Nay, Aiden. She is not well, and 'twould serve no purpose tae punish her so."

"'Twould make me feel better," he grumbled.

Iona patted her arm. "Mayhap this is so, but honestly… look at her. The woman I once knew is no longer inside that body. 'Twould be better to house her somewhere in another village and hire someone tae look after her. She can then live out the rest of her days in exile."

Aiden shook his head. "You are too kind-hearted, wife."

"I can forgive her, as can you. Holding onto such hostility will only sour our own dispositions and what good could come of that? In the end she would have won, and I will not give her the satisfaction of defeating us," she stated. Aiden nodded toward the guards.

Up the stairs they went, and once Iona reached the kitchen she felt as if she could breathe clean air for the first time in a long while. The heavenly aroma of food caused her mouth to water, but before she could ask to something sent to her bedchamber, Aiden was already taking matters into his own hands.

"We need a tub sent up to our bedchamber for my lady's bath. Hot water and plenty of food so she might break her fast," Aiden ordered, whilst they continued through Cook's domain, onward through the great hall and into one of turrets to their chamber.

A flurry of activity made Iona's head spin as Aiden shooed Gregor from the room with the promise he would see his mother at the evening meal. A large wooden tub was placed near the hearth and filled with steaming water. Another bucket for her to rise was left near the hearth to keep warm. Joan, the castle's healer, made a brief visit to examine Iona's head and said, with rest, Iona should be well. Aiden then dismissed the remaining servants, telling them he would see to his wife's welfare. He bolted the door as they left.

Iona had already stripped her filthy gown from her body and Aiden held her hand until she sank into the warm soothing water with a heavy sigh. She never thought a bath could feel this good. Aiden began feeding her tidbits of food until she laughed and said she could feed herself. He then handed her a bar of soap and a cloth, and she began to scrub the grim from her skin. Once she was clean, she stood, and Aiden poured water from the bucket over her head to rinse the suds from her body.

He wrapped her in her robe, scooped her up at the knees and carried her to their bed, where he tucked her in under the coverlets. He kissed her lips and she lifted her hand to rest upon his cheek.

Aiden gave a heavy sigh. "Please forgive me for not coming sooner."

She leaned forward to kiss his lips before she snuggled her body next to his. "There is nothing to forgive, my dearest husband." She began to try to get him to remove his tunic but instead he held tight to her hand.

"You need your rest," Aiden said in a soothing tone, whilst taking the coverlet and tucking her in again.

"But I want you…" she said suppressing a yawn.

"And I want you, but later… We have the rest of our lives together. Rest… sleep… the morrow will bring with it a new day for us to explore to our hearts content," Aiden whispered before he began singing her a Scottish lullaby he must have learned in his youth.

The baritone of his song rocked her into a gentle sense of

security that all was right in her world. With her husband's arms around her, she took solace in the thought that he would protect her and Gregor to the best of his abilities. Dunborough had its new laird and she a husband she could love for all time. She smiled in contentment and fell asleep in her husband's loving arms.

# EPILOGUE

*Berwyck Castle*
*One Year Later...*

Children's laughter, mingling with the sound of the surf hitting the shore, proved that all was right in the world. Aiden walked hand in hand with Iona through the water's edge whilst Gregor played with his cousins in the distance. 'Twas the first time in many a year that all the MacLaren siblings were together, and he rejoiced that they had been able to make this trip to his homeland. Despite Aiden pleading his allegiance to Scotland, Dristan had assured him that a brief trip south would be fine. Lynet and Ian were also in attendance. No one in their right mind would go up against the Devil's Dragon to lay harm to his extended family... or so Dristan had proclaimed in the missive he sent inviting them.

Their trip had an extra motive, since he and Iona wished to show off their daughter, who was but two months old. She was young for such a journey, but Amiria had insisted she must needs hold her niece. Since Aiden was not about to go against his sister's wishes—he told Iona that his twin would challenge him to prove his worth in the lists against her if he defied her—he had agreed to come south to Berwyck. The clan had accepted both Iona and Gregor into the fold, along with their newborn daughter. Still... he could not help but worry and refused to let his guard down.

"We are fine, Aiden. Stop scowling or the lines upon yer brow will be permanently etched there," Iona said, squeezing his hand. She rested her head upon his shoulder whilst they stopped their stroll.

His eyes traveled to those who sat on the beach eating and drinking their fill and making merry. "I cannot help but be concerned for our safety," he muttered, thinking they should return to the group.

"I suppose 'tis yer place as head of our family, but nothing will happen tae us, not with your brother-in-law commanding all those around him. I can understand why he is called the Devil's Dragon. I have never met someone who appeared so fierce and protective." Iona's gaze also went to his siblings and their families sitting on blankets in the distance.

He chuckled. "Are you trying to imply that I cannot protect you like Dristan could?" he teased.

"Never!" she replied, looking horrified. But the laughter she suppressed could not be contained and it bubbled over like the sweetest sound he had ever heard.

"Good!" he stated, whilst giving her bottom a playful slap

and staring into her mesmerizing blue eyes. "I would not wish you to think I am weak and unable to wield my sword to protect those I love."

"I believe the proof of the prowess of yer *sword*, my laird, is currently being held by yer sister Lynet," she teased, as merriment twinkled at the creases of her eyes.

"My... you are a saucy wench today, I see," he beamed, pulling her into his embrace. "Mayhap we should escape to our bedchamber for the rest of the afternoon." He began kissing her neck and he heard her moan in delight.

"We have plenty of time for just the two of us tae be alone together, Aiden. Ye need this time tae spend with yer family. It may be a while before ye are all together again."

"Wise, as always, my dearest wife. What would I ever do without you?"

"Become an old and lonely man?" she asked teasingly.

"Quite right, as no other woman could claim me until you fell into my life," he exclaimed before leaning forward to claim her lips in a searing kiss. Another moan escaped her, and he broke off their kiss before he threw her over his shoulder and took her all the way back to their bedchamber, where they surely would not see his family for the rest of the day.

She reached up to caress his cheek. "What still bothers ye, my love?"

She knew him so well. He turned his attention back to his siblings and his gaze automatically went to Sabina. She seemed so lost in their world and very much alone. "Sabina is but a shadow of the young girl from my youth."

Iona nodded. "She has been through... a lot."

Aiden looked down upon his wife. "She told you what happened to cause her to withdraw from those around her?"

Iona shuddered. "No woman should go through what she has endured. That she still lives is but a testament tae her inner strength. She just needs time—"

"—but the siege happened nigh ten years ago," he interrupted.

Iona patted his arm. "She needs time and will one day come around. Ye must be patient with her."

"I had hoped she would find someone she could come to love," he muttered, more to himself than for his wife to here.

"'Twill take a special man tae break down the walls she has erected around her heart. She has been hurt both mentally and physically. Her match is out there somewhere, and when the time is right, he will find her."

"You sound so sure all will turn out for the better where Sabina is concerned," he said raising her fingertips to his lips.

"Just as sure that one day ye will sound more Scottish than English," she taunted, whilst she pulled her hand from his and started walking backwards with a saucy sway to her hips.

"Ach, ye bonny lass! Ye have yet tae see me in all my Scottish glory," he teased back, with a cocky grin.

"I will look forward tae seeing *all* of ye come the eve, my laird," she laughed, before taking off in a run to claim their daughter.

Aye... mayhap Iona was right when she said all would work out for Sabina. Patience had never been one of his strong traits. However, he could do nothing but wait, hoping that his sibling would one day find the happiness he himself had found.

He headed toward the rest of the MacLaren clan and those

knights that followed him and the Devil's Dragon. All of them trusted friends and family that would lay down their lives to defend Berwyck and Dunborough's people. He lifted his gaze to stare upon Berwyck Castle rising majestically upon the distant hill. He halted his walk to stare upon the stronghold that had once been his birthright. There was no sense in reliving past memories of what could never be. He had a new life to look forward to.

With Iona, Gregor, and their wee bairn in his life, Aiden had finally found the place he had been searching for. The place to call his home. But 'twas not found within the walls of a keep or on some distant shore. Nay… home was the place in his heart where he kept his family.

Loving Iona brought Aiden the peace he needed to calm the wandering beast within. He had no need to search for some obscure place where he would at last belong. Iona was his home wherever they may travel. He smiled as his gaze travelled to his wife and children, knowing they had been his destiny all along. He began walking toward his future remembering how their lives together began with a kiss. Aye… he had found his home. He was content.

THE END

*Sherry Ewing needs your help!*

Book reviews help readers to find books, and authors to find readers. Please consider writing a review for **It Began With A**

*Kiss*, even a couple of sentences telling people what you liked (or didn't like) about the stories. Reviews can be posted on BookBub, Goodreads, and on most eRetailers websites. For links to this book on those sites, see Sherry's website at https://sherryewing.com/books/it-began-with-a-kiss/

Sherry appreciates the time you take to write your reviews and, yes, she reads them all! Thank you for purchasing a copy of *It Began With A Kiss*. Sherry hopes you've enjoyed Aiden and Iona's journey to finding love!

# AUTHOR NOTE

My Dearest Reader:

Thank you so very much for your support by purchasing a copy of **It Began With A Kiss**. I hope you enjoyed this long-awaited novel in my MacLarens series.

*How about a little history?*

*Dunnottar Castle by Walter Hugh Paton 1867*

First, let me begin by saying that my inspiration behind my Dunborough Castle (thanks to my daughter Jessica for coming up with the name) was Dunnottar in Scotland. Dunnottar is a ruined medieval fortress located upon a rocky headland on the north-eastern coast of Scotland. The surviving buildings are largely of the 15th and 16th centuries, but the site is believed to have been fortified in the Early Middle Ages.

Dunnottar is surrounded by steep cliffs that drop to the North Sea. A narrow strip of land joins the headland to the mainland, along which a steep path leads up to the gatehouse. The various buildings within the castle include the 14th-century tower house as well as the 16th-century palace.

I thought this would be the perfect place for my character Aiden to take over and I could see my character's lives unfolding as I began to weave their tale. I changed the name so I had creative license to make the castle and lands surrounding it my own.

In 1182 (a little bit prior to our story), Henry II's oldest child, Young Henry, reiterated his previous demands from the Great Revolt of 1173-1174. Young Henry wanted to be granted lands that would allow him to support himself and his household. Henry refused, although he did agree to increase his son's allowance. Henry then insisted his other sons, Richard and Geoffrey, give homage to Young Henry for their lands. Richard didn't feel Young Henry had any claim over Aquitaine and refused to give homage.

Although Henry forced Richard to give homage, Young Henry refused to accept. Young Henry then formed an alliance with some of the disgruntled barons of Aquitaine who were unhappy with Richard's rule, and Geoffrey sided with him, raising a mercenary army in Brittany to threaten Poitou. Open war broke out in 1183 and Henry and Richard led a joint campaign into Aquitaine. Before they could conclude it, Young Henry caught a fever and died, bringing a sudden end to the rebellion.

With his eldest son dead, Henry rearranged the plans for the succession: Richard was to be made king of England, although without any actual power until the death of his father. Geoffrey would have to retain Brittany, as he held it by marriage, and John would become the Duke of Aquitaine in place of Richard.

Although this bit of history will take us further past our story, I thought it was still interesting to include in this author note. Richard refused to give up Aquitaine and didn't want to exchange this role for being the junior King of England. Henry was furious, and ordered John and Geoffrey to march south and retake the duchy by force. The short war ended in a stalemate and a tense family reconciliation at Westminster in England at the end of 1184.

Henry finally got his own way in early 1185 by bringing his wife Eleanor to Normandy to instruct Richard to obey his father, while simultaneously threatening to give Normandy, and possibly England, to Geoffrey. This proved enough and Richard finally handed over the ducal castles in Aquitaine to Henry.

This was such an interesting time in history and the further research I do, the more I love it. You may be asking what I have up my sleeve for new books in my future. Next year, I'll be going further back in time with a new series: Knights of the Anarchy with Dragonblade Publishing. This series takes place when Empress Matilda (Henry II's mother) and King Stephen both claim England's throne. In a long round-about way, these books will connect my MacLaren and Knights of Berwyck series. I just know you're going to love these new characters and stories!

There are always people to thank with any novel I publish. My heartfelt gratitude goes out to Caroline Warfield and Jude Knight (also my fabulous editor) for beta reading this story. How you managed it with your own busy schedules always astounds me. I don't know what I'd so without your continued support, friendship and more importantly the sisterly bond that connects us from across the miles. I love you both!

My family's support is always appreciated, especially my daughter Jessica. She can always be counted on to help me work out the plot holes I come across or other brain storming that any story needs.

And to my wonderful readers and street team members. Your heartfelt words of praise, your lovely reviews, and your patience while you wait for the next story are so treasured. You continue to be the reason I write. Thank you doesn't seem to cover the amount of gratitude I have in my heart for each and every one of you. Never forget how much I value you and the friendship we have had over the years.

Until the next time, thank you again for reading Aiden and Iona's story. I hope you enjoyed their journey and I did them proud.

All my love,
*Sherry*

# OTHER BOOKS BY SHERRY EWING

## Medieval & Time Travel Series

### *To Love A Scottish Laird: De Wolfe Pack Connected World*

Sometimes you really can fall in love at first sight...

### *To Love An English Knight: De Wolfe Pack*
### *Connected World*

Can a chance encounter lead to love?

### *If My Heart Could See You: The MacLarens, A Medieval Romance*
### *(Book One)*

When you're enemies, does love have a fighting chance?

### *For All of Ever: The Knights of Berwyck, A Quest Through Time*
### *(Book One)*

Sometimes to find your future, you must look to the past...

### *Only For You: The Knights of Berwyck, A Quest Through Time*
### *(Book Two)*

Sometimes it's hard to remember that true love conquers all, only after the battle is over...

### *Hearts Across Time: The Knights of Berwyck (Books One & Two)*

Sometimes all you need is to just believe... Hearts Across Time is a special edition box set that combines Katherine and Riorden's stories together from *For All of Ever* and *Only For You.*

*A Knight To Call My Own: The MacLarens, A Medieval Romance*
*(Book Two)*

When your heart is broken, is love still worth the risk?

*To Follow My Heart: The Knights of Berwyck, A Quest Through Time*
*(Book Three)*

Love is a leap. Sometimes you need to jump…

*The Piper's Lady: The MacLaren's, A Medieval Romance (Book Three)*

True love binds them. Deceit divides them. Will they choose love?

*Love Will Find You: The Knights of Berwyck, A Quest Through Time*
*(Book Four)*

Sometimes a moment is all we have…

*One Last Kiss: The Knights of Berwyck, A Quest Through Time (Book*
*Five)*

Sometimes it takes a miracle to find your heart's desire…

*Promises Made At Midnight: The Knights of Berwyck, A Quest Through*
*Time (Book Six)*

Make a wish…

*It Began With A Kiss: The MacLarens, A Medieval Romance (Book Four)*

Sometimes you need to listen when your heart begins to sing…

**Regency**

*A Kiss For Charity: A de Courtenay Novella (Book One)*

Love heals all wounds but will their pride keep them apart?

### *The Earl Takes A Wife: A de Courtenay Novella (Book Two)*

It began with a memory, etched in the heart.

### *Before I Found You: A de Courtenay Novella (Book Three)*

A quest for a title. An encounter with a stranger. Will she choose love?

### *Nothing But Time: A Family of Worth (Book One)*

They will risk everything for their forbidden love…

### *One Moment In Time: A Family of Worth (Book Two)*

One moment in time may be enough, if it lasts forever…

### *Under the Mistletoe*

A new suitor seeks her hand. An old flame holds her heart. Which one will she meet under the kissing bough?

### *A Mistletoe Kiss* in the Bluestocking Belles boxset *Belles & Beaux* (2022)

All she wants for Christmas is a mistletoe kiss…

### *A Second Chance At Love*

Can the bittersweet frost of lost love be rekindled into a burning flame?

### *A Countess to Remember*

Sometimes love finds you when you least expect it…

*To Claim A Lyon's Heart: Lyon's Den Connected World*

A gambler's bet. A widow's burden. Will one game of chance change their lives?

You can find out more about Sherry's work on her website at www. SherryEwing.com and at online retailers.

# SOCIAL MEDIA FOR SHERRY EWING

You can learn more about Sherry Ewing at these social media links:

**Amazon Author Page:** http://amzn.to/1TrWtoy
**Bookbub:** www.bookbub.com/authors/sherry-ewing
**Dragonblade Publishing:** https://www.dragonbladepublish ing.com/team/sherry-ewing/
**Facebook:** www.Facebook.com/SherryEwingAuthor
**Goodreads:** www.Goodreads.com/author/show/8382315. Sherry_Ewing
**Instagram:** https://instagram.com/sherry.ewing
**Pinterest:** www.Pinterest.com/SherryLEwing
**TikTok:** https://www.tiktok.com/@sherryewingauthor
**Twitter:** www.Twitter.com/Sherry_Ewing
**YouTube:** http://www.youtube.com/SherryEwingauthor
**Newsletter Sign Up:** http://bit.ly/2vGrqQM
**Facebook Street Team:**
www.facebook.com/groups/799623313455472/
**Facebook Official Fan page:** https://www.facebook.com/ groups/356905935241836/

# ABOUT SHERRY EWING

Sherry Ewing picked up her first historical romance when she was a teenager and has been hooked ever since. An award-winning and bestselling author, she writes historical and time travel romances to awaken the soul one heart at a time. When not writing, she can be found in the San Francisco area at her day job as an Information Technology Specialist.

*Learn more about Sherry where a new adventure awaits you on ever page:*
**Website:** www.SherryEwing.com
**Email:** Sherry@SherryEwing.com

www.ingramcontent.com/pod-product-compliance
Lightning Source LLC
Chambersburg PA
CBHW022141240626
47153CB00007B/2459